A Tangled Web

A Tangled Web

Web

Alqamar Malik

ISBN: 1530668271
ISBN 13: 9781530668274
Library of Congress Control Number: 2016905171
CreateSpace Independent Publishing Platform
North Charleston, South Carolina

"Oh, what a tangled web we weave when first we practice to deceive"
-Sir Walter Scott

For Dad

CHAPTER 1

———

"SHUT UP . . . JUST SHUT THE hell up!" Tammy screamed ferociously as she stood up quickly, balancing her anger against the table's edge. A soft hush came over the crowd. In an instant she had become the center of unwanted attention. She felt the heat of embarrassment tearing through her cheeks. Darting her eyes quickly from forehead to forehead, daring herself not to look into all those curious eyes upon her, out of fear of her soul being scorned.

Tammy reached down and snatched her high heeled shoes up one by one from the cold marble floor. She'd taken them off minutes earlier; her soles tired from all the dancing. Stuffing both stiletto straps in one hand and a fistful of her long silky dress in the other, she shot him one last hate-filled look before storming out the room.

Tre kept his cool as he watched the back of her head. He was secretly ashamed of himself for arousing such emotion in her. Tammy practically ignored him the entire night. He hated that she never gave him attention. He went out of his way to extract it from her, adorning her with niceties, catering to her whims, giving her the attention other girls there dreamed of having. He wanted her eyes to soften when they looked at him, just once. But he may as well've been a tiny brown spot on a large brown stain for as much as she noticed him.

Despite this Tre found himself desiring her more than he'd ever desired another woman in his life. His chest heaved as the door slammed shut loudly behind her. He stood up from his chair, grabbing his half empty glass of champagne off the table, raising it above his head he spoke to the crowd,

"Never mind the drama people. Carry on! Carry on!" As if on cue, the DJ started a new song, one of the popular hits off his artist's new album as chatter began filling the room again.

"Why do you antagonize her like that?" Tammy's friend Crystal demanded in a hushed tone as she walked up behind him. Tre whirled around to face her, still in full actor mode. A boyish grin plastered on his chiseled clean-cut face. He stared back at her, one of those long uncomfortable stares, looking *through* her long enough for his mind to contemplate what had just taken place. He ignored her question, instead he leaned in and gave her a quick peck on the forehead and whispered through clenched teeth.

"Check on her for me will you Cryss?"

"You need to stop it Tre!" Crystal rolled her eyes up at his 6-foot frame as she walked off to go in search of her friend.

She found Tammy sitting alone in the cold empty stairwell, which was such an unwelcoming place compared to the sprawling recording studio they'd just left. She looked totally out of place sitting there in her beautiful gown. Crystal walked over and sat down beside her friend of twenty years. "Tamm, don't let him get to you, you know he gets off on this type of stuff." Crossing her bare legs at the knees where her pencil skirt stopped, she allowed her knee to touch Tammy's thigh in comfort. "*He's such an ass hole!*" Tammy scowled through her anger.

"Well, when you ignore him all night what do you expect?"

"I expect him to get over it!" Tammy snapped back.

"Tamm look at me."

Crystal stood up, taking a step down on the staircase so she was standing directly in front of her.

"Listen girl. That man is head over heels for you and this is the only way he sees fit to gain your attention! He's as stubborn as you are, and he's determined to gain your attention one way or another! Won't you just give him a chance to…"

"Give *him* a chance? *his* arrogant ass?" Tammy spat the words from her mouth as if they were spoiled milk. "I wouldn't *dare* give him a chance. That'll just be a train wreck!" Crystal shook her head as she giggled at her friend.

"I swear you guys were made for each other. Do you know he can't even go on a decent date? Anybody he takes out who knows of you leaves him frustrated because all he ever wants to talk about *is you*!" Tammy looked up at Crystal, a perplexed look on her face.

"Yes, *you*!" She said, cocking her head to one side and placing a hand on her hip. Aisha told me she was all excited when he asked her to meet him a few weeks ago. She went out and bought a new outfit just for their date. She said when she got there, at Mike's spot, all he wanted to know about was *you*. Aisha said he was like a mad man with all his questioning. He wanted to know "who you was workin with?" Who you was seeing? Why you didn't come to the last awards show? Aisha said she was so mad she left before even finishing her meal. It was an interrogation girl!!!" Crystal laughed as she stepped up from the stairs, making her way to the stairwell doorway. I think he called for her just so he could find out the scoop on YOU!"

"He's obsessed with the thought of you."

Crystal's last words were barely spoken; they oozed from under her breath, just loud enough for Tammy to catch a hint of jealousy in them.

"Well I aint going back in there. I'm not . . . I'm going home." Crystal sighed as she held the door open for her friend.

"*Taaaam-meeeee*" she pleaded. "*Why you leeeeea-vin?*" A look of defeat on her face.

"Get my clutch for me Cryss, Tammy ignored her plea. I left it in there on the chair. I need some air, I'll meet you out front." Crystal knew her friend all too well, she knew there would be no convincing Tammy to change her mind. Once she set it to a thing, there was no easy way to convince her otherwise.

Crystal walked back into the party, as her friend headed for the elevator. Crystal was disappointed. She always had more fun when Tammy was around. Despite this fact, she had no intentions on leaving, not just yet. As long as there were available men strolling around the room, Crystal was going nowhere, no time soon.

She maneuvered her way back through the thick crowd, noticing some handsome onlookers near the recording booth. As she passed them she swayed her hips a little more than was necessary. When she reached the cocktail table, she noticed Tammy's small clutch wasn't dangling off the back of the chair where she'd left it. Tre stood nearby with his back turned, Tammy's clutch folded under his arm. He was chatting with a guy Crystal had her eye on all night. Feeling more frustrated that ever, Crystal walked up and poked him hard in the back with her finger.

"Gimme my girlfriend's clutch!" she said firmly. She wanted him to recognize that she was tired of being the go between, but also respecting the value he bought to her own life. She and Tammy were friends long before meeting Tre. They were all friends now, but her loyalty resided with her best friend. Tammy could care less that he was some big shot music producer, but Crystal reveled in his fame. She enjoyed the recognition of being in his tight knit circle. Both women benefitted greatly by the fame attached to him, so she treaded lightly...

"Tre why you always messin with her like thaaaat?" she said coyly, curling her lip into a sly grin. He looked at her and then quickly above her head, scanning his eyes across the crowd.

"Where she at?" He asked, a slight hint of concern in his voice...

"She's leaving *thanks to you*...so give me her bag." Crystal exposed her palm toward his chest.

"Where'd she go? He asked, setting his disappointed eyes back on her.

"She's downstairs, waiting on me to bring her bag, so she can go."

Tre thought about what had transpired and felt bad. In an effort to gain her attention he pushed her away. The last thing he wanted was for her to leave.

"I got this" he said, slapping Crystal's hand away playfully.

"Hey man, ima check you a lil later bro," he turned and told the guy he was initially chatting with.

"Cryss, keep my man company" he said, pointing a finger in the guy's direction as he headed towards the door. "*You aint gotta tell me twice*" Crystal mumbled as she moved in to take the empty spot Tre had just abandoned...

———

Tammy stood outside near the entrance to the lobby of the tall story building. She was leaning against one of the massive columns that landscaped the front contemplating what Crystal told her in the stairwell about Aisha. It was a chilly night, chillier than normal for an early September in New York City. Tammy reached down to fasten a loose strap on her shoe, not noticing Tre walking towards the door. He got to the front entrance and stood there for a few seconds watching her. One of the spaghetti straps on her dress slid gently down her smooth mocha chocolate arm, exposing her bare shoulder to the evening moon. He would've love to have walked over and slid it back up for her, but he knew she wouldn't dare allow it. So he took her all in from a distance. His eyes taking their time across her body. A few strands of her thick curly locs tumbled loosely down her neck from the pin up they were styled in. His eyes moved onto her curvy waist and landed on her perfectly shaped back side. Feeling eyes penetrating her skin, Tammy looked up to see it was him.

"Whyyyy!" she murmured in aggravation. Standing straight up and raising her palms to the sky. "*Whyyy* do I have to see your face again *toniiiite?*"

He stepped out the door grinning slyly, extending the purse out to her. "Look, I'm sorry, Slim. I didn't know you would get all sensitive and shit, you know I was only playin' around." But you ain't gotta leave. She went to take the clutch from his hand but he held a tight grip on the other end. He stepped in a little closer to her. Wanting to be nearer, even if it was just for a moment, even though she was pissed at him . . . *again*! He still felt an overwhelming desire to be close to her. "You gonna accept my apology, Slim?" He asked in a sexy tone, so low she could barely make out his words.

Their eyes locked, and for a split second she felt something. Tammy yanked the bag from his fingers, turned and started down the steps. "Get a life, Tre!" she said, not bothering to look back. He stood there grinning to himself as he watched her walk away, thoroughly enjoying the thrill of the hunt.

CHAPTER 2

———

CARLOS ROLLED ONTO HIS BACK, the rickety bed squeaking alongside his every move. He lay there looking up at the ceiling, his long slender body taking up the entire length of the bed. His thoughts went to the night before. He was angry at himself for allowing his boss to keep him on such a short leash. "This shit gotsta to stop," he said aloud. He wanted to go to the album release party his buddy Reds invited him to, but he allowed his boss to force him into staying late with her at the warehouse, *yet again*. He breathed a heavy sigh, covering his head with both hands, contemplating how he'd get out of this tangled web he'd placed himself in. He knew things were getting out of hand with his boss when she began calling him from her home late at night. "I'm calling just to hear your voice" she'd say. He tried reasoning with her several times about their... *fling* being designated to the job site only, but she'd cut him off in mid-sentence every time. "I pay the bills around here young man, remember that!" Carlos knew it was a real threat. He needed his job and she knew it. He didn't have other opportunities beating down the door at him and she capitalized off this. She held the carrot out on a stick in front of him, just out of reach. He had created a monster and couldn't figure out how to place it back in its cage.

Carlos told Reds the day before that he'd meet him at the album release party that night. No soon as he hung up the phone with him, Ms. Neffie, his boss came strolling into the back loading dock. She searched around to see if any of the other guys were around. Satisfied they were

7

alone, she walked up behind Carlos, squeezing his butt cheek. Carlos wheeled around and the first thing to hit him was her cheap perfume.

He took a step back to prevent from choking. "What you doing back here boss, can't you see I'm working!" Walking away as he spoke, he hoped she'd take the hint that was as strong as her perfume and leave him alone. She followed him over to the sectional sofa where he was wrapping it for the delivery truck. "I know you're working but I needed to tell you, I want you to stay a little late after work tonight." Carlos reached down and grabbed one of the corners of the sectional, hoisting it onto his muscle-bound shoulder in one quick swoop. Walking past her, he said, "I can't… not tonight."

"What do you mean you can't?" she said frowning. Moving her head out the way so as not to get hit with the chunky furniture on his shoulder.

"I can't Ms. Neff," I already have plans. Besides what your boyfriend got to say about you spending all these late nights here at the warehouse?"

"You know I aint got nobody else but you boy" she said, waving her tiny hand back and forth in a swatting motion, "Don't tell me you're jealous now…huh? Well don't you worry yourself none baby cakes, this here's all yours . . . all yours!" Carlos was grateful that his back was turned, so she couldn't see him wincing. He'd grown tired of the charades. Initially, he was taken by it all . . . smitten. At the ripe age of thirty-two, she was thirty years his senior, flirty, and loaded with money. He thought *what the heck, at least I could gain some preferential treatment around the warehouse and probably a hefty raise from the whole ordeal.* But he soon realized he was getting more than he bargained for.

"I have other plans" he said firmly. "I can't stay tonight!"

She stood there in silence for a moment biting her bottom lip. She looked down at her doodoo brown pumps as if she didn't like herself for what she was about to say.

"Well, if you don't see any need to stay late tonight, I don't see any need to put you on the schedule for next week."

"Aww come on Ms. Neffie, come ooon! We aint doin this shit again!" he said, slamming the sectional down harder than necessary onto the trucks bed.

Just then Tom, another employee came walking in the bay area from the front, whistling a tune playing from his earphones. He stopped at the desk where they kept the customer transfer papers and began putting on his work gloves. He looked up and noticed Ms. Neffie standing near Carlos looking uncomfortable. "Oh hey Ms. Neffie, whatcha doing back here?" None of the employees at the warehouse knew about her and Carlos's rendezvous, except for the cleaning man who came in twice a week. And *he* would not have known either if it weren't for the loud moaning noises coming from her office late one night. He recognized Carlos's work jacket hanging from one of the hooks near her office and put two and two together. When Carlos went to retrieve his jacket that night, the cleaning man passed him in the hallway. He smiled at Carlos, giving him a sly look, "bet she'll sleep good tonight, huh?" he said. Ms. Neffie made up some excuse as to why she was there in the bay that made no sense to anyone as she hurried off back to her office. Carlos knew he had to adhere to her advances if he ever expected to make payroll next week.

He lay there in his bed the next morning, wondering what he could do to prevent her from damn near raping him all the time, and still keep his job. Just then his cell phone rang. Leaning his head toward the cheap plastic night stand table where it lay, he saw it was his boy Reds calling.

"Hey bro," Carlos answered groggily.

"Aye Man, what the hell happened to you last night?" Reds shouted.

"Take a wild guess"…

"Your boss?"

"Yep!"

"Got damn bro….She on you haaaaard," Reds said laughing. Carlos couldn't find any humor in his statement, so he switched the subject.

"What I miss?"

"Awwww Maaaan Cee-," you missed the party of the *year*!" Rubbing salt into his open wound. Carlos sighed, as he gripped the phone harder out of frustration. "Who was there?" He asked. "Who *wasn't!*" All the big players were there man, I kept saying, where the hell is Cee-Los… *all night!*

"Fuck, Reds, I gotta get this broad off my nuts, she's ruining my social life!"

"Ha-haaaaaa." Reds let out a hearty laugh. "You the first dude I ever heard complain about gettin some. "You don't understand man." "This broad is wicked! She be threatening my job and shit. How the hell can I enjoy getting it when her threats be in my head the whole time? Man I hate this shit, I be wantin to quit on her azz." "Quit what?" Reds asked in a more serious tone. "Your *job*? Maaan, and then what? How hard was it for you to get that job with your record? And you talkin bout *quittin!* Man you better get that thought out your head . . . you *can't* quit!"

"I know that, I said I be *feelin* like it."

"If I were you man, I'd milk that ole hag like a cow. Take her for all she's worth! You've been trying to get your own place anyways, have her to get it!"

"Naaaw Reds, you don't understand, she's shady. Whenever I take anything from her, she be throwing that shit right back in my face, using it against me later. Naaaw I don't want nothin from her at this point, except my job.

"Man, if she leanin on you *this* hard, lean on her ass back! Threaten her and say you're gonna tell her old man or something."

"She aint got no old man! That should've been my first clue."

Reds thought about it for a second . . . "well if she fires you, you can always sit back and collect unemployment, ha-haaaa!"

"Whatever man, I see you on joke time early in the morning. What's up?"

"Man I met this chick name Crystal last night. Hella-fied body! We was rapping it up, come to find out she got this friend who's in the industry. She's a....ah...a core-ah-gerfer.

"A Choreographer?"

"Yeah...Yeah...that shit!"

Carlos chuckled at his longtime friend. Reds was never one for pronouncing words properly. He had a brilliant mind, just don't ask him to pronounce any words longer than three syllables.

"Anyways, she be creating routines for music videos and stuff." She was the one who did that spot for Nab and his crew. Remember that one?"

"Ah aaah that song "Rude Dude?" "You mean the one with them dancing in suits on the roof of that building?"

"Yeeeeeah booooy that's it!!! That's the one! She did that shit son! I heard she was *all* that! The go-to for all the hot shit! I was tellin Crystal about your skillz, she thought ya'al should hook up."

"Hook up for what Reds? I aint got no money, shit like that cost money. I aint even got no label. I need to get on first. And if she all like that, she gonna want some serious cash anyway."

"Man I aint saying meet her for no video shoot! I'm saying meet her for *the connects*! She's *in* the business son, she might be able to help *you* with some connects fool!" Carlos thought on it for a second longer, not feeling the least bit encouraged, he shrugged his shoulders. "It couldn't hurt...I guess."

"Alright bet, ima call Crystal now and see how she can hook this thing up."

"O.K., but don't make me out to be no charity case Reds, I can't stand it when people be thinking I'm a charity case."

"Aw man, stop your whining . . . I got this!!!" Reds hung up in his ear, which was a ritual they'd shared amongst each other ever sense they were teenagers.

It came about when he told Reds the story about his father being murdered when he was only nine. "It was spooky Reds," he told him. "My dad called me and said, 'son, if something ever happens to me, take care of your mother, you hear me?' I knew something bad was about to happen because I never heard him talk like that before. He was like, 'Carlos you be a strong man for your mom and don't ever let anybody tell you that you aint somebody special. You have special talents son, you use them you hear me? Use them up don't you dare take them to the grave . . . use them UP you hear me!' He made me promise him that I would be somebody. Crazy thing is, Reds, I didn't even know what the hell he was talking 'bout. And then he said, 'goodbye son.' I mean, it was the way he said it, it sent chills down my spine. The next morning they found him in the alley behind the gambling house, a single bullet to his head, shot execution style. They never did find out who killed him, but moms knew what it was all about. One day, soon after the funeral she was in her room laid across the bed in the dark crying. I heard her from the hallway so I walked in the room and sat down on the edge of the bed. I aint know what to do so I just sat there. She was just lying there sobbing, uncontrollably. Finally, after a while she said, 'Carlos, don't you ever gamble, you hear me, don't you *ever* gamble!' Shit I didn't even know what the heck that was at the time . . . I just knew whatever it was, if it made her cry like that, I aint want no part of it. I was never convinced it was cancer that killed my moms, I think she died of a broken heart. She was never right after pops got killed."

After Carlos shared that story with his friend, Reds never said good-bye to him again. It wasn't discussed, it was never agreed upon; Reds just took it upon himself to never say goodbye to him ever again.

CHAPTER 3

———◆———

TAMMY SPRINTED ACROSS THE ROOM doing a double back flip. The bottom of her soles landing perfectly upright on the floor. Out of breath she turned and faced her students, "that's how I want it showing up on camera guys, I need you *high* in the air... okay??? *Synchronized*! Let's do it again, this time higher . . . *hiiigher*," raising her voice sternly.

"Music!" She pointed in the direction of one of the young dancers posted up in the corner. Obeying her command, she pressed the play button on the loud boom box. The same song repeated for the umpteenth time. "Louder, louder turn it up" she said, fanning her arms in an upwards motion. The music went up several notches as all eyes in the room watched hers intently for their starting cue. Tammy took a few steps back, moving out the way of what was soon to be flailing arms and feet. Bobbing her head to the beat of the music . . . "one and a two and GO" She shouted at them. On cue they began again, ten robotic slinkies, moving their bodies in ways most people found unimaginable. "Kick up," Tammy shouted, watching their feet intently. "Move your feet Danny," she shouted, singling out the weakest link. "Get em up Danny... up uuup!" She watched them closely as they moved in sync to the rhythm, halfway pleased with their performance.

She was in her element. Ever sense she could crawl, all she wanted to do was dance. Tammy's grandmother, a dancer herself, recognized her talents early on and convinced her son to place her in classes when she was only five. Tammy excelled. Every dance instructor who had the pleasure of coaching her, and there were many, assured him that his daughter was a natural. "She has a gift," one would say "she moves effortlessly," said another . . . Tammy mastered every genre. From Ballet to Latin to Jazz and Swing, Tammy excelled at them all!

But nothing got her feet moving like Hip-Hop. From the moment she was introduced to hip-hop, Tammy knew she'd met the love of her life. During high school, she dropped all other dance classes and focused solely on hip-hop. By the time she reached her senior year, she'd mastered the art so well that she was offered a full scholarship to Alvin Ailey's. One of the top performing arts schools in the country. She was so excited she could hardly contain herself. She couldn't wait to tell Nana, her biggest fan. The day Tammy received the acceptance letter, she decided to take her grandmother out to lunch for the news. After a light lunch of soup and salad, Tammy took out the letter she was brandishing in her purse the whole time. She carefully handed it across the table to her grandmother as if her future depended upon it. "Here Nana," she said giddily, "*read this!*"

What is it? I can't see this, chile. Nana said in a frayed voice that matched her senior years. Nana reached over, picking up the reading glasses from the corner of the table where she'd laid them earlier, after reading the menu. "Let's see what this's all about." she said. She unfolded the crisp white paper in her hands and began to read. Eventually her eyes grew as wide as saucers. "*Oooh Tammy! Ooooh, my precious Tammy,*" she stuttered, her fingers trembling. Nana was Tammy's favorite person for so many reasons. She was her dearest friend, mother and grandmother all rolled in one. Tammy's own mother left when she was just three years old.

The story her father tells is he went to bed one night and his wife was there; when he woke up the next morning she was gone. No note, no suitcase, no explanation, no nothing! For months he frantically searched for his wife. He knew she had never gotten used to being a city girl. She spoke repeatedly about wanting to move back to Africa, her home. But Sam wouldn't entertain that option. He shot the idea down every time she spoke it up, which was often in the days leading up to her disappearance. The authorities were convinced that she was alive and well and had gone back to Johannesburg, her homeland. After weeks had passed without hearing a peep from her, Sam came to the daunting conclusion that they had to be correct. He went to his mother, to ask if she would keep Tammy while he went in search of her. But Nana was successful in talking him out of the idea. She watched her son slowly deteriorate for more than a year; she knew that even if he found her alive and well, this would not mean better days for him. Nana figured whatever the reason for her leaving her precious child behind, no man would induce her otherwise. So, Nana convinced her only child to let it rest. As desperately as Sam wanted his family back together, he knew deep down his mother was right. So instead of flying halfway across the world on a wild goose chase, he packed up his wife's belongings and gave it all to the Salvation Army. He gathered all of their photos together, with the exception of a few he kept with Tammy included, and burned them. The only evidence left of her existence in his life was his daughters' chocolate brown face.

Nana was there for them through it all. She took on the mother role that Tammy never knew. It was Nana who taught her how to tie the neatest bow in her shoes, how to give a perfect curtsy, and what it meant to be a strong black woman. She instilled Tammy with the self-confidence she needed to fuel her dance career. Tammy owed everything to her grandmother. She was forever grateful for the sacrifices Nana made for her.

"I'm *sooo* proud of you Tammy," she said reaching for a napkin from the table; tears of joy streaming down her face.

They closed out the dance session, as was customarily done, in free style mode. Despite Tammy's stern look, she was pleased with how far they had developed in the routine. She knew they would be all set for the video shoot in two weeks, as long as she could prevent any of them from injury, they would do just fine. She looked up at the clock on the wall and saw it read nine o' seven. "All right, it's quittin' time." "I need to see more from *you*, Danny, and work on those lifts, all of you." "Thanks Lovey," she smiled at her music assistant as she unplugged the boombox. "Good job today guys, I'll see you all tomorrow."

Tammy walked out the room into the one across the hall as she waited for the dancers to gather up their things. Crystal would be there by nine-thirty, so she had a few minutes to spare. She walked over to the far end of the room where a floor to ceiling mirror covered the wall and grabbed hold of the brass railing extending out from the mirror as she studied her reflection. She lifted one foot up over the railing. Feeling a tinge of pain rush through her lower tendon, she reached over to massage her ankle. She began bending and straightening her knee over and over, looking around the room at all the accolades hanging from the wall. There was hardly any free space left from all the rows and rows of trophy's and plaques and framed photos of celebrities she'd worked with over the years. Tammy was proud of her success. She wiggled her toes as she scanned the row of photos, memories of each flashing back in her mind. Her eyes stopped at one in particular. One of her and Tre back stage at the music awards show. Right before the photo was snapped, he was called to the stage to accept the "best musical album of the year" award. She was so excited because she worked on three of the videos from that top selling album. She stood there jumping and clapping with excitement as Tre walked past her on his way to the stage. She recalled how he surprised her by reaching over, grabbing her hand and pulling her with him up on stage. She was so shocked and nervous she didn't know what to do. He went through his entire acceptance speech as she stood there smiling with blinding stage lights in her face, not knowing how to react. After his speech, he looked over at her with a silly grin on his face and said, "this here' young lady is my secret weapon, she's the best choreographer this industry has ever seen!" "Give it up for Tammy Johnson!" The crowd went wild as Tammy stood there in shock. Not knowing what else to do she graced the audience with an even wider smile, giving them one of Nana's famous curtseys. He then placed his arm around her waist and walked off with her back stage where paparazzi stood waiting in the wings. Looking now at that photo of the two of them up on the wall, she had to smile. Although he was the biggest pest she ever did meet, she owed a lot of her success to Tre. After that awards stunt, her career took off like a rocket! When she got to the office the next morning, there were twenty six messages on her answering machine, all from assistants of different producers and artists wanting to collaborate with her. In an instant, her name became the most recognized one for the hottest choreographed work in the industry.

"Tammeeeeee!" Crystal's voice jolted her back to the present. "I'm in here girl," she shouted back, pulling her leg down from the bar and giving it one last good stretch. Crystal joined her in the room, looking back at one of the dancers she passed in the hallway. Watching him pull his shirt down over his tight six-pack frame.

"Who the hell is *thaaaat*" Crystal whispered as she gave her friend a quick hug.

"*Thaaat* is somebody's child!" Tammy said, mocking her.

"Well 'one woman's child is another woman's pleasure' principlllle," Crystal said, twirling her neck and snapping her finger. Both women laughed. "Look at you hottie, where you been???" Tammy asked, looking her friend up and down.

"On a *date!*" Crystal said placing both hands on her perfectly aligned hips. Crystal wore a sexy cream colored dress with red stiletto's and a shiny red handbag. She swiped her fingers through her short spunky hair, adding more flair to herself.

"You look like a million bucks," Tammy said, stretching her legs some more. "Ooh those are them shoes we both liked, from the magazine . . .they're *cayuuuuute*",

Tammy said, slapping her girlfriends arm in excitement. "So where'd you go and with *whom?*" Tammy asked her as they headed towards her office near the front of the studio, waving goodbye to the last dancer as he walked out the door.

"Well I met this guy last night at the party."

"Wait…what? And you went out with him *already*? *Tonight!*"

"Well we talked on the phone and he was free tonight and so was I, so we decided to do dinner." "Don't be looking at me like that just cause *you* aint had a date since dinosaurs roamed." Crystal teased light heartedly. Tammy rolled her eyes as she reached for her sweats folded neatly across the back of her office chair. "He's a real gentlemen girl, I met him at Ray's bar and grill. We had a good conversation. He's from Harlem too, so we got to comparing different stories and land marks and come to find out we went to the same middle school! He was there several years before me though. He's a cool guy, I had a good time." Crystal plopped down in the chair across from Tammy's desk, crossing her legs at the feet as she waited for her friend to finish getting dressed.

"What does he look like?" Tammy asked, taking her ballet slippers off and putting on her socks and sneakers. "He's not *all that*" she said. "I mean he's not *ugly*…he's got a pretty smile, but he aint gonna win no beauty contests." They both chuckled. "Story of your life," Tammy said. "He's got to be around five nine or ten because I noticed he was about two inches taller than me when he gave me a hug goodbye. He's light skinned, but I guess I can get over that too. You *know* how I loves me some chocolate! I like his style though. He seems very considerate. He pulled my chair out and opened the door for me. I like that. Shoot who cares how he looks if he keeps *that* up!" Crystal laughed at herself, clapping her hands together in excitement.

"Well I'm glad you finally had a date that went well. I was starting to worry you were running them all off with your smart mouth."

"Now wait a minute," Crystal said, "you know these guys love the sass, they *love it*!" she leaned forward in her chair and frowned her nose up in Tammy's direction. "Oh Tamm! before I forget, he has a friend who's a starving artist. Some guy he grew up with. He wanted me to ask if you had time to meet with him."

"Meet him for what?" Tammy said nonchalantly, bending down again, this time to tie her shoe laces.

"He thought you might be able to give him some advice, you know, about breaking into the industry."

"And let me take a good guess"… Tammy said, standing up and placing both hands on her hips. You agreed with him?"

"Oh Tam what's the *haaarm*? Who knows, he might even be cute."

"The harm is that I don't have *time* Crystal! You know this already!"

"You shouldn't be like that" Crystal shot back. "You remember how hard it was for *you* to break into this industry. Remember what your instructor told you when you graduated? Hmmm? Don't forget to reach back. Hmmm? When you meet your goals, pull some folks up and help them meet theirs. Remember that speech?" Crystal knew Tammy was a sucker for charity cases, she took full advantage of it.

"Give *what* Cryss?? I aint got nothing to *give* him!"

"*Whatever Tammy*, you know some folks who might be able to help him, you know you do. Just talk to him at least, it couldn't hurt."

"Come on… I'm ready," Tammy said, ignoring her friend's last words as she reached for the keys on her desk to lock up the studio.

CHAPTER 4

———————

"CONCRETE JUNGLE PRODUCTIONS" TOOK UP the entire forty-first floor of the beautiful Hearst Tower in midtown Manhattan. When Tre decided to expand his successful production company, moving it from Dallas, Texas, to New York City five years earlier, he knew he needed a space that would inspire his growing list of talented artists. He understood the importance of first impressions. Perception meant everything in the music world, so he spared no expense when it came to leaving an impact on his clients, drowning out the competition on impression alone.

Tre ate, slept and breathed music. He turned a portion of the floor space into his own living quarters, which was modest compared to his sprawling work space. Everything was top of the line, from the black marble floor to the oval shaped glass enclosed sound booths that looked like something straight out of a Jetson's cartoon. To enter the booths, you had to flick a wall switch that released a metal latch on the floor, which allowed the glass doors to open automatically. When they opened, they made a *swoosh* sound, imitating the feeling of stepping into a time machine. Once inside, you had a magnificent view overlooking the city's skyline. He worked tirelessly to make sure Concrete Jungle was the biggest name in the industry. And with top charting artists lining up to sign on, it was!

Tre sat at the sound board listening to a beat he'd been working on through his byerdynamic head phones. Listening intently to the vocals coming from one of the glass enclosed booths. Growing frustrated, he sighed and looked down at his classic Patek wrist watch. He punched a button on the keyboard and spoke firmly into the pin mic in front of him. "Sherry baby, time is money, you got five minutes to get this thing right."

Sherry was a new artist. Her manager Kyte, pulled every string in the book to get Tre to look her way. After months of trying to secure an appointment, Tre finally agreed to meet with him. Agreeing only because he grew tired of his pestering more than anything else. He gave Kyte five minutes to pitch his girl. They sat there together in his office, a CD of Sherry playing in the background. Kyte listed off all the reasons he thought she would be the next Beyonce'. Tre was not at all impressed with the voice, he recognized at least a half dozen other artists in it. He knew right away that it would not be her voice that sold albums. But her look . . . her look told an entirely different story. Sherry was a bombshell! Tre sat there flipping through her portfolio, listening to the music but carefully studying each photograph. He found himself drawn into her dark brown eyes and smooth mocha skin. Her pretty face gave way to a pair of voluptuous lips. They curled up in a way that summoned you in for a kiss. Her full bust line curved into a slim waist and opened back up to reveal a perfect oval ass. Her legs went on forever. Tre found his body reacting to a strong desire to meet her. He understood full well there was a market out there for a body like hers. He gave Kyte some excuse to bring her into the studio the next day, and the rest is history.

But Tre was constantly reminded of why she'd never be a mega star. He used every trick that he knew to cover her weak vocals, he was beginning to run out of patience. "Let's make some magic here Sherry! Give me all you got or go home!" he said punching the mic button again and starting the music over from the top. Sherry was nervous, this was her first big break and she could sense it beginning to slip from her fingers. She wiped the sweat from her brow with a shaky hand, her heart was racing a mile a minute. They were on the seventeenth take, and Sherry had given each one all she had. She didn't know what else she could do to satisfy him. The pressure was mounting. She wanted to cry, but knew that would do her no good. Tre had a reputation for being tough so she knew crying would only make matters worse. Instead she closed her eyes, took a deep breath and belched out the song, leaving it all on the recording booth floor. She kept her eyes closed during the entire song. Opening them only after the music fell silent. She found his eyes staring at hers from across the room and when they locked, she knew he was not impressed. He waved his hand in a motion directing her to come out of the booth. Sherry was somewhat relieved to feel the cool air from the room on her hot skin as she opened the door to step out. She lifted the front of her pink cotton tee shirt, using it to wipe the beads of sweat from her forehead. Tre watched her as she walked across the floor in his direction. Looking down at her exposed belly he caught a glimpse of a diamond naval ring as it sparkled from the light overhead. His eyes took her all in as she stood a few feet in front of him.

"What am I gonna to do with you?" he asked, his voice matching the soft look in his eyes. It was her beauty that warmed him. "I can't make you a star Sherry, *you* got to do that yourself." Her eyes welled up as she attempted to hold back the tears. She kept hearing Kyte's voice in her ear... "Don't you be crying to that man, he's not like everybody else Sherry...stop being such a softy!" He'd say. But his words in her head were drowned out by the sound of her grasping for air as tears began streaming down her face. Tre watched her, intrigued. Normally, he wouldn't stand for it. He despised soft people, male or female. He figured if you were soft enough to cry about his decisions, you definitely weren't fit for the cold, cruel world of mainstream music. But for reasons even he wasn't sure of, he watched her intently, unmoved by her tears.

"Tell me what to do Tre?" she pleaded. "I promise I can be whatever you want, just tell me what to do?"

Tre knew it was hopeless, he knew her first time in the studio that it was hopeless, but he allowed her to continue to come back any way. He was drawn to her physical beauty. He'd worked with many attractive women, but it was something about her rare beauty he found hard to resist.

He chuckled, crossing his thick muscle arms, exposing the outline of his firm chest underneath his silky-thin shirt. He lowered his head as if defeated. "I swear you're a piece of work" he said under his breath.

Sherry knew there was one last route left she could take. She wiped the tears from her cheeks and took two steps forward, placing both her hands on the arm rails of his chair, she leaned in until their noses were almost touching. "Tell me what to do" she said in a soft sensual tone. Tre felt his manhood rise. He unfolded his arms, placing them on his knee. He shifted slightly in his chair to accommodate the bulge coming from his jeans. She peered down and noticed instantly what his movement was all about. A sly grin crossed her pretty face, she knelt down on both knees in front of his chair and began unfastening his belt.

CHAPTER 5

CARLOS WALKED OUT OF THE probation office feeling like a modern day slave. Squinting from the glaring sun, he reached in his pocket for the five dollar pair of shades he purchased from the street vendor on his way there, placing them over his eyes he walked casually down the street toward the train station. He thought about the conversation he just had with his probation officer and felt a jolt of heat climb up the back of his neck. Carlos hated not being in full control of his life. And he hated even more that he had to answer to some "white man" about his every where-a-bout. Carlos was released from prison more than two years earlier, yet he still had to visit Lancy's office on a weekly basis as if he was some cold-hardened criminal. They had him conduct another random drug test today. Never mind he hadn't *used* drugs a day in his life. Nothing on his record indicated he was a drug user, nothing. He sold plenty drugs in his past, but he was never one to get high, it just wasn't his style. Despite this he was forced to piss in that little plastic cup whenever they felt the whim to make him. As he sat waiting on the test results he already knew the answer to, he tried talking to his probation officer. He asked him about a work release program he'd heard about from his old celly when they spoke over the phone the other day. But as usual, Lancy brushed him off. The flimsy papers on his desk held more value than the life sitting right in front of him.

"All those programs are full," he said coldly, never once taking his eyes off the papers on his desk.

"May as well continue doing what you're doing, there's no guarantee you'll get into any programs even if spaces *do* become available."

He was nasty for no reason. It was obvious he hated his job, and he took it out on anyone who crossed his path. He took pleasure in shooting down hopes and dreams.

Carlos wanted nothing more than to tell him to his face he was a "fat, lazy good for nothing cracker!" But he knew an outburst like that would only succeed in getting him more time on paper. Instead he sat there, like a good negro, plucking make believe lint from his sweats while Lancy wrote whatever he saw fit to write about him in his file. Carlos wanted to travel to D.C. to visit his sister. He hadn't seen Anye since his release date. She drove up and gave him some new clothes and money that she'd collected from the folks at her job. She was his only sibling, although they were eleven years apart, they shared a close bond and he missed her. When Carlos initially asked him for permission to catch the bus down to see her, Lancy shot that down too, "that doesn't sound like a good idea," he'd said. Carlos asked why not? And he never even bothered to give him a response. He kept on writing as if Carlos never said a word.

Carlos was in an ugly jam. He hated his job, he didn't like where he lived, he despised having to come here every week, and he felt trapped. The one ray of hope he hung onto was his music. He knew he was talented. Anyone who ever heard him spit knew it too. Carlos's only dream in life was to be a successful music artist. He wasn't sure how he would do it, but he knew he could. He held onto the dream of it being his only ticket out of blood-sucking hell.

As he descended the stairs to the train platform, he thought about what he'd wear later. He initially planned to use his day off to put some rhymes to paper he had mulling around in his head. Instead, Reds had set up a dinner meeting with the choreographer lady, he thought the change in plans might be better time spent. He figured Reds was just trying to get in good with her friend, so he thought, what the hell, he'd be doing a friend a favor. Carlos began free styling as he walked up the block to where he lived. He was flowing to a beat he had in his head. As he neared the rickety brownstone where he rented a room, a loud noise cut sharply into his rhythm. It was coming from inside the house. He strained to listen as he walked up the steps to the front door. He recognized the voice as the landlord's girlfriend. He placed her mouth on the list with all the other things he despised about his life. Her voice grew louder as he turned the key inside the door knob, wishing at that moment he had someplace else to go. Carlos stepped into the living room where they were. His landlord, Fred was sitting on the dilapidated couch looking intently at the small TV that was propped up on one of the dining room chairs. His girlfriend was standing over him yelling harshly into his scalp. Fred acknowledged his presence by giving him a quick fist pump in the air. She never missed a beat, she continued yelling something about him being out late last night and not answering her call. Carlos wanted no parts of it, so he nodded to him and continued up the squeaky stairs to his tiny room at the corner of the house.

After nearly an hour had passed and she hadn't stopped her yelling, one of the neighbors called the police. Normally Carlos didn't like when the police came around, but this time he was grateful to whoever had called. He listened from upstairs as two cops ushered her out the front door, relieved he would finally be able to hear himself think. He looked down at his pad and realized he'd only written four lines. He grabbed his cellphone, looking at the time, he had less of it than he initially thought to get dressed and meet Reds. Since the house was back to a normal volume, he figured he'd take advantage of it to jot down some more lines before getting dressed.

———◆———

Reds looked down under the table at his watch for the third time in sixty seconds, his foot fidgeting from nervous energy. This was his first time meeting Tammy; he didn't know much about her except for what he gathered watching her videos, but looking across the table at her now he knew she was pissed! Crystal wasn't that much happier. Glancing over at him, using body language to speak. She kept giving him wide eyed looks as if to say, "Where is he?" He'd respond by shrugging his shoulders back at her.

Crystal was trying everything she could to reassure her friend, but Tammy was not having any of it. She sat there in deafening silence. Arms crossed at her chest as tightly as her lips. Her neatly manicured eyebrows curled in a deep frown. The waitress came over *again* to ask if they needed additional time to order.

"Not me! Tammy snapped, "I'm out of here," she said getting up from her chair. You two have a nice dinner, I'm leaving!" Crystal looked sharply over at Reds as if to say, "*Do something* quick!"

Just then a tall cup of sexy came jogging in the front door of the bar. Carlos scanned the restaurant, recognizing Reds stressed face at one of the tables near the far end of the room. Moving swiftly he headed towards them just as Tammy grabbed her purse to leave. Out of breath, he walked up behind Reds' chair, grabbing him by shoulder,

"Hey man I'm here . . . Sorry I'm late guys," he said, flashing an uncomfortable smile at them all, revealing two rows of perfect white teeth. Crystal and Reds both held their breath, they waited for Tammy's reaction. She gave Carlos a quick once over, she couldn't help but to notice he was sexy. But sexy or not, she was still heated. "Sorry alright" she said angrily.

"You had us sitting here waiting on you for almost an hour, who the hell does *that*....really?" Crystal stood up from her seat only because she didn't know what else to do at that moment. Carlos was intrigued. He looked Tammy up and down slowly, taking in her words, completely amused that such a beautiful vessel could omit so much fury. He gave her eyes a long hard stare, after seemingly forever, he asked her in a collectively cool tone,

"Where you going?"

"Out of here!" she spat as nasty as she could muster it. She turned to reach for her handbag sitting in the empty chair beside her, the one allocated for him.

"Tammy!" he said her name as if he owned it, hold up a sec... please." "At least allow me the opportunity to explain myself." She looked up at him and contemplated what her next move should be. He sensed her hesitation and walked confidently behind her. He grabbed the back of her chair pulling it out from the table, and stood there patiently, waiting for her to sit down. Tammy wasn't sure what it was about that simple gesture, but it intrigued her. She was not prepared for this type of response and was quite impressed with his even temperament. She went totally against everything her ego was shouting and accepted the seat.

Carlos reached over the table, "you must be Crystal?" he said, extending his hand out to shake hers.

"*The one and only!*" Crystal said in a relieved tone, accepting his firm hand shake. Carlos then leaned in and gave Reds the five fingered dap over the table, which gave Tammy an even clearer view of his frame. He had on a stylish blue cardigan with a crisp white shirt underneath. His brown short brim hat was a perfect match against the sweater. Carlos grabbed his chest with both hands, looking down at himself,

"I take complete responsibility for holding you guys up. I got caught up in my craft and neglected to keep a proper eye on time. On top of that, the train I was on coming here broke down and we had to get out of that one and wait for another one to come. My phone is dead, no charge," he said, pointing at it saddled on his hip. "I had no way of contacting my man to let him know I'd be late." He was mainly focused on Tammy, but he then looked around the table including everyone in on his grand finale.

"Find it in your hearts to forgive me, please, I beg of you!" He took his seat right next to Tammy's and placed both elbows confidently on the table, exposing two powerful guns. Tammy and Crystal gave each other a look. Tammy felt a brief sensation that allowed her to know she'd be enjoying this evening after all.

———

After a cordial dinner, Crystal suggested quietly to Reds that they head over to the bar for a cocktail, giving the other two a chance to talk amongst themselves. Tammy and Carlos were so focused in on each other, they barely noticed them move from the table. They sat cater-cornered, legs almost touching, totally in each other's space.

"I'm supposed to be helping *you* along with your music career, how then are we here talking about *me?*" Tammy asked him, unable to contain her wide smile. "Because *you* are a lot more interesting than *me!*" he responded. Matching her smile with his own. "I'm so glad you decided to stick around, you've made my night.

"When are we hooking up again?" he wanted to know. Tammy was in heaven. She wanted nothing more than to see this fine specimen again. She was surprised by the ease of their conversation, it felt like quality time with an old friend.

"I don't know, I'm pretty busy at the studio" she told him, drifting back into reality she thought of all the coming things she'd already committed herself to.

"What if I came there, to the studio, when I get off tomorrow? I can help you with your dance routine?" He entwined his fingers and began doing the wave with his arms.

Tammy laughed so hard she almost fell out the chair.

"Okay . . . okay." You can come if you promise me you'll *neveeer* do that again!

Carlos was on a cloud, he hadn't felt this good in a long time. He and Tammy were an instant hit. He was giddy with excitement about seeing her again. "I gotta go," Tammy chuckled as she reached for her cell phone, checking the time. Carlos stood and scanned the room looking for Reds. He was so caught up in Tammy's eyes he had forgotten all about Reds. He spotted the two of them at the bar. "Come on," he reached down for Tammy's hand, grabbing it confidently, "let's go get those two."

CHAPTER 6

———◆———

WINTER BEGAN WITH A BRUTAL whip across the face. The lake-effect snow took no mercy on any soul in its path. The weather forecast predicted snow all week long, snow on top of the freezing ice that was last week's forecast. Tre stood at the window of his studio, looking down at all the tiny huddled masses wobbling to and fro in oversized clothing. He hated winters in New York. He'd never gotten used to them, he thought about how nice it would be to hop on a plane and head to Dallas where the weather was sure to be more pleasant than this. He hadn't seen his mom in over a year, and he knew she'd be elated if he popped up on her. But it was all just wishful thinking. He had a caseload of projects to finish and there was no way he could escape them . . . not anytime soon. Tre made a mental note to call his mom later, before he went to bed. His thoughts turned to Tammy, who was fresh on his mind after seeing her yesterday. He was more convinced than ever that he *needed* a woman like her. She was everything . . . smart, beautiful, classy, ambitious, and support-ive. He fantasized often about her meeting his mom for the first time. She'd been leaning on him lately about starting a family of his own. He couldn't speak to her more than five minutes without her bringing the subject up.

"When are you gonna take time to find yourself a wife Trevor?" she'd ask him.

"All those guys you hang out with can't do nothing for you that a good woman can. You'll be forty your next birthday son, it's time you started a family, don't you think?" He knew she had grandchildren on the mind.

He'd spotted Tammy at the ice skating rink the day before; he was in the back of his limo staring out the tinted window as his driver sat at the traffic light. He knew instantly from her smile it was Tammy. He told his driver to quickly pull over to the curb, while he sat there watching her through the window. She was with a guy he'd never seen before. He watched them as they skated around the rink, over and over again. He watched as this stranger held her tightly around the waist, protecting her from the icy cold ground. He'd see him lean down and say something in Tammy's ear and she'd toss her head back in laughter. They appeared to be enjoying themselves. Tre was surprised at how envious this made him, seeing her laughing like that.

Finally, after what seemed like forever, his driver mustered up the nerve to say something. "Hey boss, we'll get a ticket if I stay here much longer." Tre knew he was right, he knew he had no business spying on her for as long as he did, but he couldn't help himself. Every time they skated his way, closer to the car, Tre's heart skipped two beats. He was worried she'd see him, watching, but he could not bring himself to look away. He was madly in love with her.

———◆———

"*Tre come here please.*" Sherry's soft voice snapped him out of his state of reminiscence. For a brief second he had forgotten she was even there. Feeling frustration grow, he kept his eyes on the small ant figures below.

"*Are you ignoring me?*" She raised her voice a little higher but just as sweet.

Tre breathed heavily, he was growing tired of Sherry. He'd given up thinking she'd ever make it in the industry, even with her beauty she just didn't measure up. She didn't have that star material. So their business relationship morphed into one of brief sexual rendezvous.

Tre turned to make his way over to the leather couch where he'd left her. During his distraction, she'd managed to remove her clothes, revealing bright red lingerie that mimicked lickerish. She lay against the soft sheep throw cover. The yellow tint in the throw accentuating the red from her bra and panties. He watched as she stroked the fur, allowing it to move gently back and forth through her fingers. Sherry knew she could only hold his attention long enough for sex, so she milked every second she could get. She arched her back and opened her legs, inviting him to do whatever he desired with her.

Tre's eyes were locked on her fingers though. Something about the way they stroked the fur excited him. He bent down and began using his tongue to lick them one by one, back and forth, matching the rhythm of her caressing the fur. He took his hand and cuffed one of her breasts, squeezing her nipple aggresively, he whispered, "After this, ima need you to leave." Sherry felt the pain of his words go straight to her heart as it stopped for a brief moment. She thought about ending it all right there. Getting up from there and scraping her pride up off the floor. Instead, she left it right where it lay and allowed him to remove her panties...

After their couch charade, Sherry gathered her things and headed for the door as Tre began opening the small boxes containing CD's that were piling up in the incoming mail bin beside his desk. She reached for the door knob, but something came over her. Instead of leaving she turned and walked swiftly over to where he sat. "I'm not coming back until you learn to give me some respect, Tre!" Using a stern voice and pointing a perfectly manicured finger in his face. Tre was anticipating this reaction sooner or later. He knew women, so he was not surprised. He sat back in his chair, holding a half opened box in one hand. He gave her a long hard stare. "That sounds like a fair trade," he told her casually.

"What do you mean a fair trade?" She demanded. "What are you saying?"

"If you have to ask for respect, then you're in a weak position to begin with."

Those words cut her more deeply than the previous ones. "*Kiss my ass you fucking bastard!*" She shouted before turning and heading for the door again, tears welling up in her eyes.

Tre sat there in his wide office chair, unmoved by it all. For him it was just another sad day for another sad girl who got in too deep. After she had slammed the door behind her, he reached over and picked up his desk phone, punching the one button that rerouted him straight to the front desk. "Yes Mister Davis!" His assistant who sat downstairs in the lobby answered on the first ring. "Hey Barbara, I'm expecting a couple of investors to come through; they're not on the roster for today's meetings but they're cool to send up when they get here. Hey, and do me a favor, if you see her again, don't let her up unless I say so okay?" Barbara knew exactly who this "she" was. She'd seen her come and go on several occasions. As a matter of fact, she'd seen a lot of 'em come and go over the years. It was always the same look of determination on all of their faces going in, and the beat up look of defeat coming out. A revolving door of broken hearts.

"Yes sir, you got it!" Barbara said just as Sherry stepped off the elevator wiping a tear from her face. The two women locked eyes for a brief moment, as Barbara placed the phone back on its receiver. Sherry sensed something was strange by the way Barbara looked at her. She slowed her pace and stopped right in front of her desk. It was a hunch, but a strong one. Sherry gave her a look that could kill a dead man.

"Was that him?" She demanded. Surprised Barbara looked around the room as if to suggest there was someone else there she could have been speaking to.

"*Was that HIM!*" Sherry repeated, growing angrier. A few extra seconds passed before Barbara responded.

"Yes!" Barbara said, giving her the answer she desperately wanted.

"What did he say?" Sherry demanded. Barbara gave her a look of pity. She did not want to add any more pain to what Sherry was obviously already feeling.

Sherry leaned forward and slammed both hands down on the desk so hard that it shook.

"*What the fuck did he say?*" She shouted, anger welling up and forcing its way out through her eyes. That action startled Barbara, she was a sweet old lady who didn't take well to being confronted. She leaned back in her chair, away from Sherry and spoke in a cracked voice. "He said if you came back, not to let you up." Sherry was floored. She felt as if Barbara had just thrown dog feces in her face. She stood up straight and spoke firmly, "*You tell that arrogant son of a bitch, he aint gotta eeeva worry about me coming back here!!!*" And with that, she stormed out of the building like a hurricane.

CHAPTER 7

CRYSTAL LAY ACROSS TAMMY'S BED with one arm propped up against her head. She watched Tammy as she struggled in the bathroom mirror with her hair. "Shit, this aint working for me" Tammy said sighing frustratingly. She placed both hands on her hips allowing her jet black locks to go tumbling down to her shoulders. She was preparing for another date with Carlos who wanted to take her to a one-man show some guy he knew was performing at the Apollo, but her hair would not cooperate. Crystal chuckled as she watched her struggle. "See, I told you long time ago to cut all them troubles off your head!" Glad I had enough sense to," she said pulling at one of her own reddish bronze kinks she wore in a short cropped natural. "I just oil it, twist it with my fingers and go! Look at you over there, strugglin." She said snapping her finger at Prince bellowing out from the radio.

Tammy took the brush she was holding and slung it playfully in Crystal's direction who swatted it away in just enough time before it hit her upside the head. "Girl hush, you know I adore my locks. It's just tonight – I aint got time tonight to be foolin and *YOU* are my hair stylist and won't help me!"

"Oooh no chile...I done told you before, when I leave that salon, my fingers go on strike. They be saying no mas...no mas..."

"You're so mean to me, Tammy told her, but ooooh there's always a plan B!" She headed for the closet where she kept the plastic bin full of hats and scarves.

"Pleeeease don't tell me you're gonna wear a *hat*?" Crystal asked in disgust.

"You watch me!" Tammy said as she rummaged through the bin in search of one to match the jumpsuit she was wearing. She settled on a red flapper styled hat with a tiny peacock feather peeking out the side.

"Now the trick is getting all this hair underneath it" she said, walking back to the bathroom mirror to attempt the magic act.

"So you really like this guy huh?" Crystal asked, more to strike up conversation than to hear the response she already knew was coming.

"*I doooo*" Tammy cooed giving her hips a little sway to drive the point home.

"I'm glad you guys hit it off. Wish I can say the same for me and Reds."

"What happened with that anyways?" Tammy asked, stopping what she was doing to come and sit on the edge of the bed, giving her friend her undivided attention.

Crystal shrugged her shoulders nonchalantly. "We just weren't compatible I guess."

"What makes you say that?" Tammy asked, pressing her for more information.

"We were both searching for things in each other that just weren't there. I mean, it wasn't any one particular thing I can put my finger on, we just aren't compatible." She thought for a second before adding, "for instance, he liked to stay at home watching movies all the time when I preferred to get out and be more active. Or like, like, he eats pork. Tammy took that moment to frown her face up into a ball. And you *know* I can't stand that. That's a *huge* no-no! He would complain that I have too many male friends. Every time we were together and my phone rang he would roll his eyes at me."

Crystal poked her bottom lip out, making a puppy dog face.

"You *do* have a lot of male friends Cryss", Tammy said. "Well, I can't help it if people love me." Just then Crystal's cell phone rang. It was laying in the middle of the bed where they both were able to read the name on the screen; it was "Joe" calling. They looked at each other, bursting into laughter. "See there, that's the kind of stuff that's gonna *keep* your ass single." Tammy got up from the bed and headed back to the bathroom mirror.

Crystal hit the end button on her phone, not bothering to answer. "I can't help it if the men like me." Confirming her own sex appeal, she raised one of her long legs up in the air, twirling her ankle round and round. "It's not like I'm screwing any of em."

"Yeah but how was he supposed to know that?" Tammy asked. "Put yourself in his shoes."

"Eeew you just reminded me that was another thing, his feet used to smell sometimes." Tammy laughed hard at her friend. "Girl I swear you are a mess."

"Enough about my loser love life, what about you and *Ceee-Looos?*" Crystal sang his name, readjusted her body, getting more comfortable on the bed. Tammy's eyes lit up at the mere mention of him.

"Whew! Girl that man does something to *meeee.*" I mean Cryss, I aint felt this way about a guy sense Troy in high school. Remember Troy?"

"Yeah I remember Troy. You were sick in love with that boy; you and every other girl in school."

"Gosh don't remind me. But I feel that way about Carlos. That young teenage love. I'm enjoying him, he really caters to my feelings. He's really into me; how I feel, what I like, what I want, you know. He's very giving of himself."

"What about his background?" Crystal asked. Tammy gave that some thought before she answered.

"You know what Cryss, to be honest, I haven't even thought that much on it. It's crazy because if he were anyone else, and I found out that he was an ex con with no real stability, I'd run like hell. But I like him. I truly like him a lot."

"That's all sweet and dandy," Crystal said sarcastically, "as long as he's not looking for a free ride in the back seat of *your* taxi."

"Naaaw, I don't get that at all from him," Tammy said quickly and confidently. "I'm no pushover, besides I can gage pretty fast if somebody's just out for a free ride. It's hard to fake your true intentions for long; it's been four months. There's something special about him."

"Aint nothing wrong with that," Crystal said in an understanding tone.

"Aint nothing wrong with that until *Tre* finds out!"…She reiterated. "And then all hell's gonna break loose!" Crystal sat up swiftly on the bed, checking Tammy's face for a response. Tammy grew angry at the thought that Tre would sabotage what she and Carlos were growing.

"I wish he would!" Tammy spat as she jammed her hand into her makeup case, grabbing her favorite tube of lipstick.

"Giiiiirl, you and I both know that Tre is gonna flip his lid when he finds out about you two," Crystal said, contemplating the possibilities. Tammy sucked her teeth at that, and gave it all some thought as she rolled the soft pink lipstick across her lips.

She hated the demands Tre placed on her. It was obvious how he felt about her, but Tammy couldn't understand why she had to be a participant in *his* feelings. She was grateful for all the success his status brought to her own life, but she didn't see why she had to keep stepping lightly around him.

"And please don't say he'll just have to get over it 'cause you and I both *know* that he won't!" Crystal said in the most serious tone she'd used all night. "Remember what he did when he saw that guy slip you his number that time we were hanging out at Mike's spot?" "Remember that?" "He had security grab that poor dude by the back of his neck, and threw him out the club!" Tammy shook her head in shame as she remembered that night. Tre had no problem throwing his weight around.

Tammy knew what Crystal said held merit. She was more concerned for Carlos than herself. She knew Tre was not removed from making Carlos's life a living hell.

"Well, he just won't ever know that's all." Tammy said feeling defenseless.

"Just don't mention anything to him or any of his artists about us, okay Cryss?"

"I'm the *least* of your worries!" Crystal shot back.

"Sometimes I regret the day I ever met that bulldozer." Tammy said walking over to the tall cherry wood jewelry box that stood beside her bed.

"I don't" Crystal said playfully.

"I *know* you don't," Tammy grabbed a pair of silver hoops and began placing them on her ears.

"I thought you were helping Carlos with his music. What happened with that?"

"Nothing happened, I'm still trying to figure out the best way to go about it," Tammy said bending down and opening another drawer that contained all the bracelets, settling on a pair of silver bangles.

"Tammy! We both know the *only* person who can help that man out is Tre. And if you like him as much as you say you do, then you *have* to help him."

"That's my whole dilemma Cryss, of course I want to help him, but Tre is so unpredictable. I don't want to be thinking I'm helping him only to be leading him into the lion's den!" Crystal thought on Tammy's words before she responded.

"Yeah...you have a good point."

"I'm still working on it, Tammy said. The right opportunity hasn't presented itself yet."

CHAPTER 8

———◆———

CARLOS WAS AT THE BOILING point. He was so angry he could hardly contain himself. His boss couldn't have picked a worse day to trouble him with her freaky desires. He paced the warehouse floor, cell phone in hand, contemplating what he should do. His first thought was to just quit. He considered going into her office and tossing his work gloves onto the desk. He wanted nothing more at that moment than to be rid of her for good. But common sense got the best of his emotions. He knew that quitting now would only make matters worse for himself. He needed his job now more than ever, now that he had someone special in his life. He checked the time on his wristwatch, his thoughts turned back to Tammy. She was expecting to meet with him in an hour. He purposely waited to call her in hopes that he could get outta his boss's trenches. But his plan didn't work. She was as stubborn as a mule, set on having her way.

Carlos stopped his pacing and went and sat on one of the plastic covered couches. He thought on what he'd say to Tammy. He knew she'd be disappointed, he hated to disappoint her. Besides that, he was looking forward to spending time with her. He hoped this wouldn't tarnish what they were building. He dialed her number on his cell phone and began tapping his foot nervously as it rang in his ear. Tammy answered on the second ring.

"Hey you!" she said in that peppy voice Carlos had grown to adore.

"Hey baby, I'm sorry to disappoint, but I have to change our plans tonight." He figured he'd just get it out quick no chasers.

"Whyyyyy? what's wrong?" Tammy whined, sensing the frustration in his voice.

"I have to stay a little later than I expected here at the warehouse. I won't be done in time enough to meet with you and still get to the theatre before the show starts."

"You don't *have* to come here first Carlos, I can meet you there?"

"Naaaw, don't do that." Carlos said lowering his tone. He was smitten at the fact that she really wanted to see him as much as he wanted to see her.

"I'll make it up to you baby, I swear I will."

Just then he heard his boss's footsteps making their way over to where he was. He knew it was her from the flopping noise her patent leather pumps made on the cement floor. She always wore shoes too big for her feet, so they made this double flopping sound when she walked. He didn't want his boss to know anything about his personal life, especially about Tammy. He knew she'd only make things worse for him if she knew he had someone in his life he cared about.

"Tammy, I gotta go, I'll call you later. Okay, I promise baby." he said hurriedly. He hung up before she got a chance to say anything more. He stood up quickly, bracing himself as if preparing for a battle.

"Who was that?" Ms Neffie asked, in a tone that left no question who was boss.

"None of your business!" he shot back as he made his way out of her presence.

"Where are you going?" she said, chuckling at his last statement.

"What do you want Ms Neff?" he stopped, turning to face her.

"I have something for you." She handed him a long rectangular box with no labeling on it. Carlos's curiosity got the best of him so he took it from her and peeled open the top. It was a long pink vibrator, still in the package. Carlos gave her a long hard look of disgust.

"You are pathetic!" he said, shoving the box back into her arms. Ms Neffie burst into laughter. She laughed so hard her glasses almost fell from her face.

"What's wrong? You're not up for a little fun tonight?"

"Ms Neffie I'm not interested in that, I'm really not interested in *you*, I just wanna come here and do my job like everybody else."

"You don't need to keep saying that to me," now growing angry. You probably got some young cunt all up your ass, that's why you don't enjoy me no more." Carlos wanted to tell her that he never enjoyed her . . . ever! But he knew it would be useless. So he kept quiet and walked off to finish his work load for the day. Ms Neffie stood there for a while longer, watching his big firm muscles expand and contract as he maneuvered the heavy furniture around. She licked her lips enjoying the feeling of what she'd been anticipating all day. She was reduced to giving him oral sex in order for him to get aroused, but she didn't care about that, she actually looked forward to that part too.

"I'll see you when you get done!" She shouted above the loud noise coming from the bay door as he pushed it open. Carlos heard her but chose not to respond . . .

CHAPTER 9

"I DON'T SUGGEST YOU PILE all your assets into this one category Mr. Davis, it's too risky. We can split them up under different trusts. We can add all of your real estate back west under a separate living trust, then place all your assets from this here business in another. I also see here that the insurance you have on your work-related equipment doesn't cover you in the event of a catastrophic loss?" Tre listened intently as his new accountant gave him the run down on his finances. He was grateful to his friend Mike for the referral. Mike owned a couple of popular night clubs around the city. The last time they hooked up, Tre was telling him about all the additional money he was kicking out in taxes. Mike told him straight out to "fire your accountant and use my guy. He's the best in town!" Mike said. "Expect to kick out some up-front cash, but he's worth every penny!" 'We call him the *balloon man,* 'cause after meeting with him, your pockets swell up like a hot air balloon" . . .

"What about this huge tax bill?" Tre was asking the balloon man. They were in his office, inside a rustic old building east of Canal Street; it sat next door to a meat packing plant. When Tre's driver pulled up to the front, he made him check the address twice to be sure they were at the right location.

"You sure man? Check it again…this can't be it!" He thought for sure a guy with his reputation would've had a swanky contemporary spot over in Soho someplace. Balloon man was a strange looking feller. A thin, white guy with loose stringy hair, so loose he didn't bother combing

it. He wore a checkered suit jacket that looked as if it were made in the sixties along with some ashy jeans that showed signs of excessive wear. When they shook hands Tre noticed a button missing at the end of his sleeve. They sat in a small room, barely large enough to fit the desk and two chairs. The walls were bare, no color, no pictures, no window, no *nothing*! Tre had Barbara gather all the papers that balloon man requested before coming. He grabbed the neat pile rubber band on his desk that morning, without bothering to look through the pile himself, he bought it all with him. They now lay sprawled all over the desk like a tornado hit the place.

"Don't worry about the tax bill," he said as he plucked one of the papers up from the desk and held it up to the light as if he was checking a bill for the security strip.

"Did you know that the IRS uses special paper to prevent document fraud?" He said more to himself than to Tre.

"They think they're smarter than me, *no one's* smarter than me!" Tre was officially freaked out. He couldn't wait to chew Mike out for not warning him this cat was a nutty professor.

"Uuuh what's my damage?" Tre asked attempting to skip the subject.

"I don't know yet. I have to pour over these forms, one by one, line by line, and when I'm thru I'll tell you what the damage is." He knew coming in that his services wouldn't be cheap, he decided to pick his battles and go with Mike on trusting this crazy cat.

"Well, what do you know, time has crept up on me." Tre said looking down at his wristwatch.

"I must be getting to my next appointment." He didn't have anything pressing on his schedule at that time, but he felt an intense need to be outta there.

"Here, just call my assistant if you need anything further, I gotta go." Tre reached into the inside of his suit jacket and pulled out one of Barbara's business cards. He kept them on hand for times like these.

"I can't take that!" the man frowned, refusing the card Tre extended him. "I speak *ONLY* with clients, no assistants! Didn't Mike tell you that?" Now Tre was *really* freaked out. He began to wonder what he had gotten himself into.

"Aaah okay man, whatever you say." He didn't know how else to respond.

The balloon man dismissed him with a wave of a hand, "I'll have you all fixed up in no time . . . go on . . . get outta here." Tre left the place feeling uneasy. He was expecting the numbers to be smudged a little here and there, as they all do, but this guy was talking "*top secret*" lingo. He was grateful to be saving some money, but he didn't want anything heavy to come down on him. He decided he'd just dial Mike up in the morning, to help put his mind at ease about the whole thing.

———

The meeting with balloon man took less time than he'd allotted so he had some to spare. He told his driver to make a stop pass Tammy's studio. He hadn't *officially* seen her sense the party and was beginning to miss her presence. He figured she was still salty about him teasing her about her mom. He never expected her to take him so seriously. He kept calling her a "no mama having self." After a few times of that Tammy screamed on him. Thinking back on the whole incident, he could clearly see he'd hit a nerve up till that point he never knew existed. He made a mental note to not joke with her about her mother. It was close to noon and he was hungry. He figured he'd try and make it up to her by taking her to lunch.

He knew she'd be at the studio so he didn't bother calling. Besides, she'd only find some lame excuse over the phone not to go if he did. As the driver pulled up to the front of her studio, Tre felt a sense of pride sweep over him. Tammy was one of the first people he'd worked with when he launched his production company there in New York. Back then she was a struggling artist and he was attempting to gain a foothold in a new city. He had a couple of strong artists who did well with him in Dallas who he'd convinced to move east with him. It wasn't hard to win 'em over, being as though he was solely responsible for making them the brand name successes they were. It turned out to be a lucrative business move for them all.

One of his artists, Shawn G, did so well in record sales that first year, they decided to take his show on the road. Tre thought Shawn could benefit from someone innovative helping to choreograph his stage routine. He deliberately wanted someone under the radar, someone with fresh new ideas that hadn't been manipulated by fame. But Tre was new in the big city, he didn't know a single soul he could call for the task. He was at his wit's end when Shawn called him up late one evening. He told Tre he was at the Lincoln center with his girl, watching one of the best hip-hop performances he had ever seen in his life! He recorded part of the show on his phone and presented it to Tre the next morning. After a few phone calls here and there, he was routed to "Bust a Move" dance studio in Harlem. Before Tre came along, Tammy hadn't done any work as demanding. He gave her her first big break in the music industry. Although her career was now a booming success, she still worked from the same modest studio where it all began. There were two large murals painted on the brick front, one on each side of the entrance way. The murals were painted to resemble hip hop dancers, one male and the other female; they were painted in a silhouette of the famous kid n play dance move. The only thing that prevented the two murals feet from touching each other was the entrance door. It was a creative concept. There was no guessing that you were in the right place to learn hip hop dance. The words "Bust a Move" were spray painted at the top of the door in big bold lettering resembling graffiti. Tre grinned to himself thinking back on earlier days. He admired her humbleness, although it was something he himself did not possess.

Tre instructed his driver he wouldn't be long. The blasting music was the first thing that hit him when he opened the door. The small reception area in the front of the building was empty. He made his way down the narrow hallway following the sound of Usher blasting from the speakers "situaaaaaations will ariiise, in our liiives buuut you gotta be smart about it, cele-braaaations." He began snapping his fingers and bobbing his head to the beat feeling the excitement of just knowing he would be seeing her face. He heard her before he saw her.

"That's it Angel! That's it girl!" she was saying excitedly to one of the dancers when he reached the doorway of the room. He stood there slightly out of view, observing the scene. There was a room full of young girls in tip top shape. Tre quickly counted about twenty of them, scattered all about. He guessed them to be in their late teens, early twenties. Some were in colorful leotards, others in shiny biker shorts. It took all he had in him not to stare. Tammy's back was turned towards the door, but she could see his reflection in the mirror in front of her. She was not surprised to see him. After five years of rocky friendship, she grew to recognize his distinct patterns. She knew he'd be making his way to her soon. She never knew in advance when or where, but he always found his way. One of the young dancers recognized him immediately and let out a low scream. "Oh my god, that's Tre!" she said, covering her mouth with both hands. Tammy flashed him a half-hearted wave through the mirror, their last encounter running swiftly through her head.

"Hey ladies, I didn't mean to interrupt your beauty session," he said leaning casually against the door frame. He folded his arms across his chest, settling his attention on Tammy. He gave her a good look over. Her locs were in a messy ponytail. She wore a cut off white tee shirt that exposed her flat as a pancake stomach. The words "Bust a Move" were spray painted in pink across the front of it. Matching sweat pants hugged her hips tightly. Her pant legs were rolled up at the bottom, exposing her tight calves. She wore nothing on her feet; her neatly manicured toes were painted a soft peach color.

"Yes you did interrupt our session," she said sarcastically, walking over to the far end of the room where she kept the sound system. She grabbed her hand towel from the back of the chair where she'd left it, and used it to wipe the back of her neck before flipping it across one shoulder. She sighed heavily, reached over and hit the stop button on the radio. The room fell silent except for a few giggles from some of the young ladies who were still smitten by his presence. Tammy glanced at the clock on the wall, seeing it was a few minutes after twelve.

"Ladies let's take a break for lunch," she said.

"I'll meet you back here in forty-five minutes. Remember NO HEAVY FOOOOODS," she shouted, as they began piling out of the room one after the other.

Tre took a step back from the doorway into the hall, giving them room to pass. He got a few winks and kisses blown at him as they fumbled their way past him into the room across the hall that was being used for changing. The same girl who screamed when she saw him went running to the front of the studio in search of something to write with. She came back a few seconds later with a red sharpie.

"*Please please can you sign your name on my arm?*" she held out the pen for him and began jumping up and down, barely able to contain her excitement. He chuckled as he took the sharpie from her hand and asked her name?

"Its Skyy . . . Skyy Tucker" she said still jumping. "You gotta hold still Skyy, if you want me to get this right" he told her. She stopped the jumping but you could clearly see her arm tremble as he wrote. Tammy peeked her head out the room to see what all the excitement was about and noticed half the class was lined up in the hallway, waiting for their chance to be smeared by a marker.

"Uh uh...nooope, nope, no, no, noooo!" Tammy said shooing them all away. "This man eats, sleeps and farts just like all the rest of you. Leave him be and go get yourselves some lunch...NOW!" She said in a firm voice. They all began moaning and sucking their teeth in disappointment as they made their way slowly back across the hall to change. Tre was secretly relieved. He rarely turned down autograph requests, especially from the youth, but he was in no mood this afternoon for a groupie session.

He finished up on Mary's arm and handed her back the sharpie.

"Looks like you were the lucky one today huh? Don't be bragging to the other girls, they'll only hate you for it," he whispered to Skyy before following Tammy down the hall into her office. Once inside she plopped down in her office chair. He wasn't sure if she was drained from her workout or from seeing him, so he asked,

"What's wrong with you?"

"There's nothing wrong." Tammy lied. She was in no mood for Tre today, but was in no greater mood for drama, so she went along to get along.

"What you doin on this side of town?" she asked him.

"I came to take you to lunch," he said in that cocky tone Tammy despised so much.

"What makes you think I *want* to have lunch with you after that last stunt you pulled?"

"Awww girl, you know I was just clownin' around. Come on, get dressed; I have the car waitin outside." Tammy suggested an Italian spot two blocks up. She didn't have much time to spare and didn't want to go too far. But she could've led him to an old dirt road at the ends of the earth as far as Tre cared. He was just thrilled to have some alone time with her.

Once there, Tammy settled on a bowl of minestrone soup and a tossed salad. She could have eaten plenty more but she would have felt bad after just scolding her students about their own lunch habits. Tre ordered a heaping bowl of spaghetti with a side of cheesy garlic bread and a large iced tea. The aroma coming from his side of the table was heavenly.

"So Tam, what projects you got coming up?" he was genuinely interested in knowing.

"I have a video I'm working on for that group the Chili Peps, and then Crystal Bell has an upcoming tour starting this summer, I'm working on some sets for her and her crew."

"Crystal Bell!!!" Tre repeated in surprise. "Wow, that's a big deal little girl."

"Well, actually I'm one of two choreographers that she's using for her stage show. I was a little offended at first until her accountant told me how much they were willing to pay. It was just as much if I were doing the entire set myself, so my ego got over that real quick." They both laughed.

"Are you living your dream?" he asked between gulps of his tea.

"Yes I am," she said excitedly, without even thinking.

"I mean, don't get me wrong, it's hard work for sure, and some of these famous bourgeoisie get under my skin with all their unrealistic demands, but I do love to dance, *and* I love to teach."

"If you weren't dancing, what do you think you'd be doing?" he asked.

Tammy took a little longer to answer that question. She put her spoon down and cupped her hand on her chin, with her elbow on the table she thought about that question deeply.

"You know, I have no idea?" she said. She shrugged her shoulders and reached for the spoon again.

"Maybe I'd been a housewife or something. I would have married some hot shot lawyer and had a house full of kids by now, probably home schooling them all, who knows." . . . She chuckled at the thought of it.

"I can see you doing that" Tre said, giving her a serious look. So serious that it made her a bit uncomfortable.

"Well, thank God for this life," she said attempting to break the spell.

"Do you *want* kids?" He asked, thinking of his mom.

"I think deep down, every woman wants a child of her own, even those who say they don't . . . I wouldn't mind a kid or two."

Tre felt relief. Relieved that he didn't have to switch up the fantasy that lived inside his head. He daydreamed of someday having Tammy as his wife, and he was grateful she too desired children.

"What if you could live both of your dreams in this one life time, would you consider it?" Tre knew he was pushing it, but he had to know. Tammy sensed where the conversation was headed. She didn't want to hurt his feelings so she shrugged off the question, skipping the subject all together.

"Crystal has this friend who's into hip-hop, he's really good. I suggested to her that she let you hear him." Tammy held her breath and bent her head, her nose almost touching the soup as she waited for his reply . . .

Tre figured she danced around his question purposely. He didn't want to seem overbearing so he let it slide.

"How old is he?" he asked.

A bit relieved, she came up for air. "Ummm if I had to guess, I'd say he was about thirty-five, thirty-six or so.

"Thirty-Six?" Tre said, raising an eyebrows.

"Isn't he kinda old to be starting a career in the music game?"

"But he doesn't look old, he's got mad skills," Tammy said hurriedly, before catching hold of the excitement in her own voice.

"So how does Crystal know this guy?" He asked. Tammy searched her brain for a good answer. She was never good at lying, and she was now beginning to regret her words.

"Ummm, I think they met on line or something, you know Crystal."

Tre thought about it for a second . . . "Tell Cryss to bring him past the studio next Tuesday, tell her to call before they come." He looked down at his wrist watch, "the clock is tickin pretty lady, chop-chop."

CHAPTER 10

———

"YOU TOLD HIM *WHAT*!" CRYSTAL shouted so loud Tammy tried covering her ears with her shoulders. They were in the middle of the shoe isle, Crystal stared down Tammy as if a person was growing out from her forehead. Tammy knew she'd be pissed. She waited as long as she could to break the news to her. She figured she'd be safe from Crystal's backlash sense they were out in public, she figured wrong.

"Tell me you're kidding?" Crystal asked, hoping what she'd just heard was some bad joke. Tammy stood there fiddling nervously with a buckle that was on one of the display shoes.

"You *are* kidding, right Tammy?" Crystal said more firmly.

"I didn't know what else to say Cryss! I mean what was I supposed to say? I couldn't tell him the *truth*." Tammy searched Crystal's eyes for a hint of sympathy.

"I can think of a *million* other things you could've said that wouldn't have implicated *ME*!" Crystal breathed a heavy sigh of frustration as she searched around for one of those portable stools the store kept in their isles. She spotted it near the end, Tammy followed her over to it.

"Now, explain this to me again like I'm a five year old" Crystal said as she sat down. Tammy went over the details of the conversation she and Tre had over lunch a few days earlier.

"So let me get this straight, I'm supposed to take *Carlos* up to the studio on Tuesday so Tre can meet him and hear some samples? And he thinks I met Carlos off an *internet dating site*?"

"Oh God, this is *bad*, this is *real bad*, Tammy. Crystal said shaking her head in defiance. There is no *waaay* I'm going through with this....I can't *believe* you put me in this."

"You were the one who kept telling me I had to *help* him!" Tammy said.

"Yeah I did, but I aint think you was gonna conjure up this crazy scheme and put *me* in the middle of it!" "What the hell were you thinking?"

"I really wasn't," Tammy gave her a sad face. But we have to go through with it now Crys, this can be Carlos's one big shot!"

"What did you tell *Carlos*?" Crystal asked her in disgust.

"*Oh noooo*" Tammy said, her eyes growing wide as saucers. "I can't tell Carlos the truth *either,* or he won't agree to it."

"WHAT!" Crystal screamed again louder than before.

"You tell me how this is supposed to work Tammy! How in the hell are we supposed to pull this off...huh?"

Tammy thought on that for a second. "Okay-okay listen . . . Tre said for you to call him before you came. So when you call, you can just say Carlos is embarrassed to let people know he searches the internet for dates, so just tell Tre not to mention it while he's there. That's it. That's all you have to say Cryss!" Crystal took a moment to consider Tammy's scheme. She shook her head in frustration as she got up to finish browsing the aisles.

"If this doesn't work, you do know that *BOTH* our heads will be on the chopping block. You *do* know this right Tammy?"

"Yeah . . . yeah . . . I *know!*"

———◆———

"It's been *four months* and you *still* aint hit that!?" Reds asked shockingly.

"Maaan, I've been knowing you for a long time son, I never guessed I'd see you like this...*Four months tho? "Sheeeeeit,* you a better man than me brah!" Carlos grinned as he stuffed his hands deep into his puffy coat pockets, the collar attached to his hood tickling the hairs on his five o'clock shadow. They were watching the little leaguers running to and fro on the damp grassy field below.

"Yeah, I never guessed I'd be like this either" Carlos said right before they both jumped to their feet and began cheering with some of the others in the crowd.

"Run...run...touchdooooown!" He and Reds gave each other a congratulatory slap of the hands as they settled back down onto the cold medal bench.

"He's growing fast, gettin tall." Carlos said, spotting Reds' son Shaheed on the field in the sea of yellow and black uniforms.

"Yeah, I'm proud of my lil man, He's got a birthday coming up."

"What'll he be like Seven-Eight?" Carols asked him.

"Nine".

"*Nine!*" Carlos repeated in surprise....Damn time sure does fly!

"How's things with you and his mom?"

"Better" was all Reds offered in response. Carlos knew Lisa was a touchy subject for Reds, so he didn't push.

"I saw your girl Crystal the other day, she looked good. Too bad you guys couldn't make a love connection, we could've had a double wedding.

Reds sucked his teeth, "Crystal's a diva, she's spoiled. Too much independence will ruin a chick."

"What ever happened to the days when woman tended to the home while the men took care of business? Nowadays things are turned upside down." Reds said as he watched his son on the field.

"Nowadays the powers that be got *both* of us grinding hard, they can tax us double time now. Meanwhile the children suffer from the lack of nourishment from both parents. This new aged stuff is *killing* our families.

"Ayyy-men to that!" Carlos said reaching into his coat pocket for his vibrating phone. It was Tammy calling. He still got a rush of excitement every time she called.

"Hey babe, what's up?" he said through the line. Just then another roar erupted from the crowd so he removed himself from the bench to take the call a little further away from the noise. Minutes later Carlos returned, a shocked look on his face. Reds noticed the change in his expression right away.

"Wassup?" he asked him.

"That was Tammy. Tre, with concrete jungle wants to hear me sample some stuff at his studio this Tuesday!"

"Are you serious!?" Reds asked sharing in his shock.

"Are you *serious* man!?"

"WOOOO-HOOOO!!!" Carlos shouted in pure joy at the top of his lungs. He was so loud that even some of the little leaguers glanced over to see what the excitement was all about.

CHAPTER 11

———————

CARLOS AND CRYSTAL WALKED INTO the office building, both full of nervous energy but for totally separate reasons. He still didn't understand why she had to be there with him. Tammy called him the morning of as he was getting dressed to say something came up last minute, and that Crystal was going to meet him out front at the studio. He tried telling her that wasn't necessary, that he was good to go alone, but Tammy was adamant.

They reached the receptionist desk,

"Hey Barbara" Crystal greeted her with a halfhearted smile. "Can you call up and let Tre know we're here."

"Sure thing!" Barbara sang as she picked up the phone's receiver. Barbara was always in a cheerful mood, today was no different.

Crystal took that moment to really check Carlos out. She stared him up and down. He had dressed for the occasion wearing some dark grey dress slacks and black penny loafers. He had his leather jacket unzipped and she noticed a red tie peeking out from underneath.

He was watching Barbara so intensely that he didn't notice her staring. Crystal felt queasy, the knot in her stomach squeezing tighter as she heard Barbara say, "Yes sir, I'll send them right up!"

On the elevator ride up, Crystal turned to Carlos, "it's best if I do all the talking okay?" Confused, he asked her *"why?"*

"I just think it'll work better for you if I talked." She said.

Carlos was offended. He didn't see why her presence was needed at all, let alone talk *for* him! He chuckled just to loosen the muscle in his jaw.

"I appreciate you trying to help, but I can speak for myself." Crystal decided not to push it as they stepped off the elevator and reached the door to the studio. They let themselves in, and Carlos took a moment to look around. He was impressed right away with all of the state of the art equipment. The place was clean as a whistle, the view was amazing! He had been to a couple of studios over the years to lay a few tracks but those places were dumps in comparison to this. The door on the opposite side of the room opened and Tre walked out. Carlos felt like he was having an out of body experience as he tried hard to contain his excitement. Crystal walked over to greet him.

"Hey Tre" she said, offering him her cheek to kiss.

"This is Carlos, also known as Cee-Los" she moved aside, allowing space for the two men to shake hands. Tre gave Carlos a longer than normal stare,

"Haven't we met before?"

"No sir", Carlos said confidently. "Rest assured I would've remembered if we ever met." Tre turned his attention to Crystal, "how's my girl?" He asked.

"She's fine" Crystal shot back, turning the subject quickly back to Carlos.

"This guy's got raw talent," she said. "You gotta hear him."

"Oh yeah!" Tre said, giving Carlos a good look over. "I'll be the judge of that!"

"Have a seat" Tre offered them both a seat on the leather couch. Crystal still felt uneasy, deciding instead to walk over and grab a magazine from the rack he kept in the lobby area. Hoping the latest version of Vibe magazine held the secret that would stop her heart from beating a hundred miles per minute.

"So what's your genre?" Tre asked as he grabbed the rolling office chair from behind his sound board, sitting down across from him.

"I do mostly conscious rap" Carlos told him.

"How old are you?" Tre asked as if he didn't already have the answer.

Carlos shifted a bit in his seat, he was hoping the question concerning his age would not come up, he knew it was a mark against him.

"I'm thirty-six. But I've drawn a lot of skill from my experiences" he quickly added. It took a lot to impressed Tre. He'd seen talent come and he'd seen 'em go just as fast. He came across some with as much flair as Michael Jackson, just to watch them slip through the cracks due to laziness or personal issues they couldn't conquer. He learned to never judge a book by its cover; he knew the game far too well to ever attempt that.

"Conscience rap huh" he asked?

"Yep!"

"Who's influenced you the most in the game?"

"Immortal Technique and Dead Prez," Carlos responded without hesitation.

"Why conscious rap? Why not follow the big money into mainstream?" Tre asked. Carlos thought over this carefully. He knew Tre was a business man, first and foremost. He understood his choice to be more conscious about what he wrote may not be in alignment with Tre's pockets. Carlos understood well that copy-cat sell outs equaled money in this game. The more you fell in line with the popular artists, the more money there was to be gained. He spoke carefully,

"Mainstream is filled to the brim with artists all saying the same thing. The wave of the future, as I'm sure you know, is returning to our center. I've made a conscientious effort to stay ahead of the game." Crystal flipped through the magazine unaware of anything on the pages, she was listening intently to every word they shared between them. She was relieved that the conversation remained on music, but she still took shallow breaths none the less. She wouldn't be able to relax until they were completely out of there.

"Are you sure we've never met?" Tre asked again, a puzzled look on his face.

"I'm sure," Carlos replied.

"You got any sounds out there now?" Tre asked.

"No...not really. I mean I've got some old stuff on track, but I've evolved sense then, so naw.

"So you're not in contract with anyone?"

"Naaaw, I'm free as a bird," Carlos told him.

"Okay....let's see what you got," Tre said standing up and walking over to one of the sound booths. He hit a switch on the wall and the glass door swung open making that futuristic sound. Carlos was in awe! He had never seen anything like it before, he felt like a kid in a candy store. He maintained as much composure as he could given the circumstances.

"That's cool man!" is all he offered as he attempted to calm his excitement.

"Step up and put on those headphones. You know how this is done right? Tre didn't wait for a reply.

"Ima play a series of beats and I want you to show me what you can do wit em...I wanna hear a different flow for every beat I throw at you. Just that simple. Got it?"

"Got it!" Carlos replied. Tre walked back over to the sound board and began turning knobs and flicking switches, preparing for the show-down. Crystal was curious, she bought the magazine she wasn't reading over, and took a seat on the couch, watching the whole scenario play itself out.

"Your ole gee boyfriend better be good, or ima embarrass him" Tre said. Crystal gave him a mug face, rolling her eyes but said nothing.

"All right Cee-Los, here we go." Tre said into the mic. He began with a slow tempo. Carlos closed his eyes and began swaying his head to the rhythm. He allowed two bridges to pass before he began. *"The killing fields, corner store schools, usin weak skills, breakin our wills, climbin no hills, pilin up bills...* Tre switched up the beat, speeding it up a little and Carlos was right there with him. He sped things up even faster and Carlos never skipped a beat. They went on doing this dance for more than twenty minutes. Carlos never used the same line twice. Finally, after an hour passed Tre cut the music and Carlos kept right on rapping . . . *"the blood in my brain movin faster than a plane, its plain, who remains, as the lame, take the train…"* Tre burst into laughter, cutting into his flow…

"Come on out man, you've proved your point!" Crystal sat there beaming as Carlos made his way out of the booth and back over to the couch. Tre was officially impressed,

"How much more of that you got in your head?"

"I can go like that for days" Carlos said unflinching.

What's your objective?" Tre asked him.

"I just want an opportunity to present what I got in me to the world. I just wanna get my words out there!" he said, jabbing a finger toward the window. Tre nodded in agreement.

"You got mad talent no doubt. Paired with the right musicality you have the potential to go far. Your age may become a factor, but your message is mature, so it may fit. You'll likely appeal to a more mature audience anyway. You got a manager?"

"Carlos chuckled at the thought.

"No." Carlos turned to Crystal, "not unless you consider those two ladies…"

Aaaw man, that was good wasn't it Tre? Crystal spoke right over him.

"What would his next step be…huh?" Tre gave her a perplexed look before turning his attention back to Carlos.

"Well, I'd first advise you to get a personal manager. Someone who knows the industry, who can cut deals for you."

"Why do I have to do that?" Carlos was anxious. Why can't we just work together on something, *you and me*?" Tre leaned forward in his chair and looked him square in the eye.

"You should *never* be that trusting of anyone in this business!" Carlos was taken aback by his words. He didn't know how to respond, so he said nothing.

"I like your style. There's something about your personality I think the public will take well to. We might be able to work something out, but I don't wanna see you back here without a rep." Carlos was so thrilled he could hardly contain himself. He tried playing it cool but all his built up energy traveled down to one leg, it kept shaking.

He placed his hand on his leg, applying pressure to it to try and stop it from trembling.

"You have anybody you could recommend?" Carlos asked him. Tre sat back up in his chair and crossed his arms over his chest. He shook his head, looking over at Crystal.

"You aint school your new boyfriend on the rules of the game?" Her eyes grew wide as saucers. She laughed looking nervously over at Carlos. Carlos went to say something but she quickly blurted out,

"It's a learning curve!" Ummm don't you have work to do? Another appointment coming in or something?" Tre and Carlos gave each other a confused look. She babbled on . . .

"I mean, he needs a manager right? So we know this is the next step. Come on," she said to Carlos standing up, "let's go get you a manager!" Carlos gave her a look as if she'd lost her mind. Tre looked down at his wrist watch,

"Matter of fact, I do need to prepare myself for this conference call." Suggesting that he was in favor of ending the discussion prematurely.

"When's the next time we can hook up?" Carlos asked him, flashing Crystal an angry look as he stood up.

"Have your new manager give me a call, she knows how to reach me." Tre nodded his head in Crystal's direction and started toward the door to see them out. As they left he reached down to kiss Crystal's cheek.

"Tell your girl I'll be back there soon for another lunch date." He gave Carlos some dap. "Looking forward to working with you." Carlos grinned and nodded in agreement as they walked out the door. Carlos reached the elevator door first, jamming his finger on the down button.

"What the hell was *that!*" Deliberately keeping his voice low so that Tre couldn't hear him from the other side of the door.

"What?" Crystal asked innocently

"What you mean *what!*" Why did you sabotage my meeting?"

"I didn't *sabotage* anything!" Crystal said defensively.

"I still don't know why you had to be here in the first place!" "I didn't need you with me no how." Carlos said angrily.

"Wow!" Crystal pretended to be surprised by his words. "Some thanks I get. I guess you could've gotten an appointment to meet with Tammy by yourself too huh? Which in turn led to this meeting, huh?" Just then the elevator arrived; they rode it down in silence. Carlos spoke as they were exiting the building,

"Look Crystal, I'm sorry. You're right. I appreciate you looking out." His was a warm heart who didn't like drama.

She smiled at him, "It's okay, good luck finding a manager!" she said right before they parted ways.

CHAPTER 12

CRYSTAL'S HAIR SALON WAS IN full swing when she walked through the door. Almost every chair in the place was filled. She was late for her first appointment messing around with Tammy and her crazy ploy. She whisked past Amina, her assistant at the front desk, waving her hand as she went acknowledging her presence in the building.

"Miss Crystal . . . Miss Crystaaal," the young receptionist covered the end of the phone with her hand as she tried catching Crystal's attention walking past.

"I have no tiiiiime," Crystal sang back keeping it moving. Crystal wore an apologetic look on her face as she hurried up to the little old lady sitting in her styling chair.

"Awww Miss Catherine, I'm so sorry for keeping you waiting. Please forgive me" she said sincerely.

"I was wondering where you were. I was just about to leave." The old lady shot back with a frown.

"I'm so sorry, I'm so glad you didn't." Crystal reached in her top desk drawer for a cape.

"I would offer you an explanation for my tardiness, but you wouldn't believe it if I told you." she said, placing the cape over her own head then reaching back in the drawer to do the same for Miss Catherine.

"Miss Crystal," Amina walked up. "That was aunt Tammy on the line, she said to call back as soon as possible please, it sounded important."

"Okay. How many people do I have waiting to be serviced?" Crystal asked her.

"You have two in the front and another one should be here in like thirty minutes"

"Aaaargh," Crystal grunted, "Ok...OKAY where's my shampoo girl, where's Tess?" She said looking around the room frantically as she started in on the old lady's head. She spotted her on the other side of the salon, chatting with another stylist.

"Go tell her to prep my next appointment. Apologize to both ladies for me and let them know I'll be with them momentarily, please."

"Okay" Amina said before taking off to obey orders. Crystal was in her seventh year of ownership. All she ever knew was hair. While all her high school classmates were prepping for college, she had other ideas. Crystal had no interest in college. She had a different plan in place.

"I don't need to pay no college professor to teach me what I already know" she'd say to people when they asked her about not going to college.

"I already know what to do." While her friends were studying *how to* books in their dorm rooms, Crystal was running a one-woman operation. She had set a five year plan for herself. Which was to stay at home with her mom and stack up every single dollar she made doing hair until she saved enough to purchase her own salon. During that time, Crystal never turned down any business. She'd work most days from six in the morning until midnight, a never ending flow of beautiful women coming through her mother's basement door. She never lost sight of her plan. Not unless you take into account the one year she got off track dating that self-centered guy who milked her for a portion of her savings. It cost her an additional six months just to recuperate from that bad relationship. After five years and six months, she'd saved up enough cash for a substantial down payment on her own salon. And to now be able to help her mother along, was a gift times two. "For all those *extra* years you took care of me." She'd say to her whenever she dropped pass for a visit.

"Alllll right Miss Cathy, what are we having done today?" she asked the old lady sitting in her chair.

"Just the usual" she said. "I think I need a trim though, I've been getting a lot more hair in my brush than usual lately."

"Let's see," Crystal told her as she grabbed her fine tooth comb and used it to pull the lady's kinky grey hair in an upwards motion. Crystal heard her cell phone buzzing inside her purse. She knew it was Tammy calling, wanting to get the scoop on how things went with the meeting this morning. Crystal rolled her eyes, she was still sorry for ever agreeing to such an outrageous thing. She was stuck in the middle of a messy situation. She finally answered after Tammy called back twice.

"*Tammy I'm flooded here at work I can't talk to you now!*"

"Okay...Just tell me quick what happened?," Tammy said.

"I am not gonna tell you quick because I *can't* tell you quick. Just know your secret is still in the bag, now I'll talk to you about the details later, when I get home," Crystal said right before hanging up in her ear.

Later that evening Crystal sat on the balcony of her condo, smoking a thin joint she kept on hand, for nights such as these. She took another drag and blew the smoke out in a steady stream from her mouth as the knots began to loosen out of her nerves. She remembered Tammy, she promised she'd call her when she got home, but at that moment she didn't want to do anything more than to just relax for a bit. She let her head rest loosely on the back of the lounge chair and began humming the words from Anita Baker's song coming from the unit next door. She thought back on the day's events and chuckled to herself. After another quick pull, she used the make shift aluminum foil ashtray to dab out the lit end. She stopped using weed for purposes of getting wasted a long time ago. That youthful stage of her life had come and gone. All she ever did these days was a quick two or three pulls, every now-and-again, just enough of a buzz to wash away some of life's stresses.

Crystal unfolded the tiger print throw cover that was lying at the foot of the chair, and used it to cover her body. It was a chilly night so she pulled the cover up to her neck and closed her eyes, allowing the music from her neighbor's stereo to engross her soul. She lay there for what felt like hours, when in actuality it was only minutes before her cell phone began buzzing in her lap. Crystal pulled the cover up above her eyes, peeking under it to see who it was. She breathed heavy seeing it was Tammy. She was in no mood to talk but knew she'd just pester her until she got through.

"Yeeeeeeeessss" Crystal dragged her voice as she answered, leaving no doubt about her frustrations.

"Crystal!" Tammy said her name like she was scolding a naughty child.

"You know I've been on pins and needles all day, why you aint call me?"

"Did you talk to your boyfriend?" Crystal asked her sarcastically.

"Briefly, but I can't expect *him* to give me no details, that's why I'm bugging you!"

"Whaaat you wannaaaaa knooow?" Crystal dragged the words out of her mouth again.

"Cryss… what you doing?" Tammy asked her in a tone that suggested she knew all too well.

"I'm chillin…why?"

"Are you on the balcony?"

"What is it to you?"

"Girl I swear…you need to leave that stuff alone."

"Did you call to criticize me?" Crystal said sassily. "Cause if you did, I'm not interested in it."

"Okay…okay, you win, just tell me what the heck happened today pleeeease."

"It's not much to tell…We got there and they talked briefly, Carlos spit some stuff inside the booth, Tre loved it and he suggested he get himself a personal manager so they could talk business. It went well, despite a few close calls."

"Whaaaat!…what close calls?" Tammy was anxious to know.

"One time Tre called him my *boyfriend*! And then another time I think Carlos was about to spill the beans about knowing you, but I diffused the situation, so it's all good. Crystal said, feeling wickedly proud of her quick wit. Your outlandish *lie* is still under wraps...You do know this is all a lie don't you?" Tammy was quiet as she took in her last words.

"Helloooooo" Crystal shouted in the phone.

"I'm listening" Tammy said quietly.

"Well say something, got me over here feeling like I'm crazy, talking to myself"

"You ARE crazy!" Tammy said jokingly. "Let me let you go cause obviously you aint feeling me tonight...Peace Cryss"

"Peace girl," not offering any resistance she said, "I'll talk with you tomorrow." Crystal hung up and closed her eyes again, pulling the warm blanket back up around her neck.

CHAPTER 13

———

TAMMY SAT AT THE KITCHEN table of her childhood home. With squinted eyes she blew softly into the cup of steamy tea before taking a sip. Her father sat across from her smiling widely. It wasn't often that Sam received a pop-up visit from his only child. He milked every minute of it.

"You used to make that same face when you were little." He said to her. "Whenever you ate something hot, you'd squint your face up just like that." He grabbed a sugar cookies from the plate in front of him, plopping it into his mouth. Her dad was in great shape for his fifty-six years. You could see the tell-tell signs of the workouts he kept up with at the gym. Her Nana emphasized to them both the importance of taking care of the body. Her father was a handsome man who was normally better groomed, but this day his salt and pepper beard scattered unruly across his face, showing signs of needing a trim. Tammy smiled back at him.

"So dad, tell me about this lady you've been seeing, the one grandma mentioned? Yaal had dinner last week? Not sure why *I* wasn't invited... but oh well, I'll get over it."

He chuckled as he took a few last chews before swallowing the cookie.

"You mean Catherine? There's nothing much to tell really. We work together, at the plant. We go out after work from time to time, just to break the monotony. I've been knowing her for some time now. She lost her husband a couple of years back."

"Oh really?" Tammy asked sarcastically. "How did her husband die?" Old reruns of the tv show *cold case files* quickly running through her wild imagination.

"A heart attack." He added.

"You introduced her to Nana, so it must be serious?" He laughed at that notion. "We old single folks are just happy to have some company, that's all. I had plans to meet with your Nana anyways, we decided to all do dinner together."

Tammy wasn't convinced; "mmm hmmm" she said cocking her lip to one side, calling his bluff.

"I'd still like to meet her. There must be something special about her if you guys been out more than once."

"What about you baby girl? He asked, switching the subject back to her. Anybody worth noting?" Tammy's grin turned into a wide smile.

"Oooooh you've been holding out on *mee* huh young lady? "Who's the guy? Come ooon spill it!" Tammy cocked her head back and laughed real hard at him.

"Why you say it all like that?" She asked.

"Who's this fellah that's got you grinning from ear to ear?"

"*He's just* my friend, we've been seeing each other on a regular basis though" she told him, still unsure how she should be addressing him.

"Her father sat up taller in his chair, intrigued by her excitement." "Oh Yeah?'

"Yeah, he's cool, I like him so far, she said."

"So far?" her father repeated.

"Yeah...so far so good, but you can never be sure about these types of things, as *you* know." He chuckled with pride at his daughter.

"So what kind of guy is he?" Tammy took that moment to take another sip of tea. She placed the mug back down carefully onto the matching saucer before leaning back more comfortably in her chair. "He's a good guy as far as I can tell, I mean, I've been knowing him about four months now, I enjoy his company. He's cool." She deliberately suppressed her true feelings in front of her father, wanting to be extra careful not to play things up to soon.

"That's not saying much. What's cool about him?"

"Ummm let's see. Carlos is funny, and smart. *Real smart*" she emphasized. "He likes to read, he's into a lot of political stuff. Conscious of the world around him, you know, I like em, he's cool." "He be telling me things all the time that I *should* know, but have no clue about," she added. "I learn stuff from him all the time. I like that about him"

"And what else do you like about him?" Her father pressed.

"He likes treating me when we go out, even though he knows I make more than him, he still never expects me to pay for anything when we're together." Tammy was saying the things she knew her dad would want to hear. It was all fact, but hand-picked facts.

"That's the gentleman thing to do," he said firmly. "That's to be expected."

"Does he have children?" He asked her.

"Nope!".... "Never been married" she said proudly.

"And school?" he was taking mental notes. "Where did he attend school?"

"No college. He finished high school but...aaaah ummmm yeah... he works a nine to five."

Tammy almost blurted out that he'd spent some time in jail, catching herself right before she said it. She didn't think it was a good time to go into that with her dad. She needed to shine him in the brightest of lights first, just for now.

"So does he work in your industry?" he asked, sensing this could potentially be serious.

"Not yet" she responded casually as she leaned in to grab one of the cookies from his plate.

"So he's looking for a job in the industry?" Her father tried guessing.

"He's an artist...well, *soon* to be hip-hop artist."

"Is that so huh!" He asked, feeling the sense of relief begin to dissipate.

"Just so happens he just signed on with Tre, they're gonna be working together. You know Tre doesn't sign on *anyone* he can't make mega bucks from.

"That sounds promising," her father said, still unconvinced. "So what happens if this *hip-hop* career doesn't pan out?"

"Daaaaaad", she became frusted. "*You alwaaaays do thaaaat, goshhhhh!*"

"Do what?" he asked, throwing his hands in the air as a sign of submission, suggesting he had no clue as to what she meant.

"Why can't you look on the bright side? And be optimistic, gooosh! What happens if things *do* pan out? Besides, I'm just getting to know him, its not like we're planning marriage or something."

"Alright, alright...you have a point" he said. Not wanting this rare visit from her to turn into a fight, he let that part go...for now.

"Well how bout this; what's he do to pay his bills while he's preparing for his *successful* music career?" She rolled her eyes at him, as she allowed her thumb to caress the handle of her tea cup.

"He works at a warehouse. A furniture warehouse, on 5th and P, not far from that ballet school I used to attend."

"The one over near Patricia Lynn's dance studio?"

"Yep, that's the one!"

"You two sound pretty serious" he said, half asking half stating.

"I mean we're dating... exclusively, but it's only been a few months, we'll see where it goes."

"Last I remembered that boy Tre was trying every trick in the book to get you to pay some mind to *him*. He even called *me* that time asking if I needed anything." He chuckled, "tryin to schmooze me to get to you.".... Guess he finally got over it huh sense he's working with your new friend now, what's his name... Carlos?" Tammy didn't respond. She just smiled softly, lowering her gaze so he couldn't see the shame in her eyes.

Finally after a long silence, he spoke.

"Hey, I have something I think you should have." Tammy's thumb froze on the mug, sensing the nervousness in his voice.

"What?"

Sam scooted his chair back and placed both hands on his knees. He sat there like that, contemplating a few more seconds longer before standing up and walking over to the drawer nearest the fridge. He opened the drawer where he kept all his mail and lifted out a postcard. Walking back over to the table he handed it to her before taking his seat again. Nervously he watched her flip the postcard back to front, attempting to figure out the puzzle.

"What's this?" she said finally. "Who's it from?"

One side displayed a colorful picture of two giraffes grazing from a tall mimosa tree. A golden sunset appearing in the background. Her heart began beating fast when she saw it was postmarked Africa. The hand written words on the back read….

Samuel, my soul is here but my heart is there. Please tell her she is thought of every single moment. I have never forgiven myself…

There was no signature, no return address. Just three heart stopping sentences on the back of a colorful postcard. Tammy wasn't sure how to react. She looked into her father's eyes for guidance or comfort or both. Looking down at the postcard and up again into his eyes. He reached out and rested his hand atop of hers.

"I wasn't sure if I should have bothered you with this or not," he said. "I thought about it for weeks, and concluded it wasn't my place to keep it from you." Tammy remained speechless. Up until that point she had done a good job of keeping the feelings she had about her mom tucked far away in the back of her conscience. She rarely thought of her, and when she did, it was always a passing one. Deliberately. Tammy was too young to remember anything much about her mom. She used to believe she could smell her though. When she was young, she remembered asking her Nana if she was breastfed as a baby. Her Nana told her "yes." But Tammy knew that already, for she remembered being able to smell her mother's scent. The stories she was told, about her mother, always conflicted (in her own mind) how selfish of a person she painted her to be. She'd convinced herself a long time ago that she was better off without her mother's presence, if she was selfish enough to leave her, then she was better off not knowing her after all.

Tammy read the note for a third time, studying the words as if they held clues.

She laid the postcard down on the table in front of her, photo side up.

"*Nice picture,*" was all she could bring herself to say....

CHAPTER 14

———————

CARLOS TOOK TRE'S ADVICE AND quickly found himself a manager. After asking around to a few of his buddies on the spoken word scene, he was able to retrieve a name and number for an Anthony Wright. Anthony made a low budget name for himself managing several C-rated artists. One hit wonders. Folks you'd have to search a name a thousand times over for in your head before being able to put a face to it. Carlos knew he wasn't the best of choices, but he was desperate and Anthony was the only one available at such a short notice. When Carlos discussed with him what he and Tre talked about, Anthony seemed more excited than he was. Carlos figured he needed an opportunity to reach the top of his game too. He thought maybe they both could have a go at it…together. Anthony seemed hungry for success. Carlos could respect that about *any* man.

All three men were scheduled to meet together for the first time that evening. When Carlos arrived in the lobby of the Hearst Towers he noticed a short, stocky looking guy resembling Spike Lee without the glasses standing off to the side. He wore a suit a size too big for his small frame, which made him appear even smaller in stature than his actual size. Carlos could tell right off he was nervous. He carried a stack of notebooks almost as tall as himself. When Carlos approached him to shake his hand, he had to quickly reach out to grab the stack before they all slipped from his arms.

"What's this?" Carlos asked curiously.

"Oh these? These are biographies, articles of my work. I brought them so Tre could take a look at them." Carlos chuckled uncomfortably.

"Shouldn't this meeting be about *me*? Why would he care about those people?" Pointing to the overgrown stack in his arms.

"Yeah aah but you see, he'll know that I have worked with other artists. I've never met him, but he has a reputation of being a tough guy. If he knows I've done this sorta thing before, he won't try and get over on me . . . ummm . . .I mean us!" Carlos just shook his head. He knew right then and there, based on first impressions that he'd be negotiating his own deal that day.

Once upstairs, they made brief introductions before Tre escorted them into his office. He was finishing up a session with another artist that went over time. As he left them sitting at his desk, to go to wrap it up, Carlos took that moment to really look around the space.

The walls were painted a light tan in color. A mural of two large music notes painted in black were on one of the walls. In one corner, behind his desk stood a bookshelf made from cherry oak. From what he could gather from the distance of his seat, the books all appeared to be music related. *The Art of Music. How to Break into the Hip-Hop Industry. Beats like the Pro's,* he read off some of the larger font titles. The black marble floor extended from the main studio into his office. The desk was the largest piece of furniture in the room. It matched the color of the bookshelf with a glass covering so shiny, it could've easily been a mirror. The desk was neat and orderly, everything on it had a rightful place. The pens lay neatly in their holder, the paper clips were in another small cup free of any dust or debris. A few loose papers sat tidy inside a ben, a sleek cordless phone took up space on the desk's edge.

There was nothing personal that he could tell in the office space. No family pictures, no hand written notes, not even curtains for the huge bay window.

Just then Tre walked in, both men sat up a little straighter in their chairs as he took his seat behind the desk. Not bothering to apologize for his delay, he gave Anthony a long hard stare before getting right down to business.

"This man has a lot of talent," Tre said. Pointing over at Carlos but never taking his eye off Anthony. "I could use his kind of skills for where Concrete Jungle is headed, so what kinda deal you got for me?" Anthony grinned nervously and took one of the bulky white notebooks from his lap. He placed it on the desk and flipped it open to its first page, turning it around so Tre could see the content from where he sat. Confused yet curious Tre pulled the notebook in closer to himself and began flipping through its pages. Carlos hung his head in shame. He didn't want to have any parts in what was about to go down.

"*What the hell is this?*" Tre demanded as he began flipping more quickly from one page to the next.

"Aaah, ummm, that there, wait...this one... that's Vaughn Shepherd." Upon hearing that, Tre stopped at one of the pages and began studying the face in the photo up closer.

"Is this the same guy that sang that song... about the bus stop? The hook about hot girls at the bus stop? "*Stop for the girls at the bus stop.*" Something like that?" He asked looking up from the book searching Anthony's face for a response.

"Aaah yeah, that's him!" Anthony said proudly.

"What you showing me *this* for?" Tre asked in disgust.

"Aaah well... he was my client, along with a few others." Anthony went to reach down for another notebook on his lap but Carlos placed a firm hand on top of it. One book was more than enough.

"So what's your point?" Tre asked, shrugging his shoulders, growing more and more frustrated by the second.

"Aaah, yeah well I thought I'd show you some of my work."

"If this is it, man I'm not impressed." Tre closed the book, handing it back to him. "Let's talk about this guy here. What we got worked up? What's the deal?"

Carlos got goosebumps just hearing the sound of that. Anthony took longer than a pause to respond, he really didn't know what to say. He had never been to a real live negotiations before so he didn't know what he was expected to do. Everyone he'd worked with up to that point were paying the *studios* for recording time. He was accustomed to the low budget end of the industry, the place where amateurs clamored for action. His main role before then consisted of him bugging the crap out of local radio stations until they'd agreed to give his artist some air play. He was known for being persistent. Most often, radio producers agreed to play a few of his recommendations during their late night hours, just to get him to stop showing up at the station.

"Aaaah ummmm, what are you suggesting, he asked?" Carlos and Tre looked at each other as if they just heard an alien speak. Carlos jumped in the conversation to save himself.

"Listen man, as I mentioned before, I just wanna spit. You asked that I find myself a manager, so I did. To be honest with you, I'd do this shit for free if I had to. Based on our conversation the other day, I can tell you're not the kind of guy who goes around screwing people over. If you did, I would've heard about it by now. Bad news travels fast. I plan to make you a lot of money Tre, no doubt in my mind about that. If you are straight up and fair with me, then put this on everything... I'll be the same with you!" Tre said nothing, allowing him to continue.

"Just give me a fair n square number man, let's put it on paper so I can sign it. Plain and simple...and let's make *history*!"

Tre was impressed. He folded his arms across his chest and gave Carlos a proud grin. He liked this guy but was cautious at the same time. It wasn't easy for folks to get close to Tre. He had a stand offish character that was difficult to penetrate. But Carlos intrigued him more than a bit. Tre looked over at Anthony.

"Well my man, looks like today's gonna be your lucky day!"

———

CHAPTER 15

REDS WAS ON PINS AND needles. It took everything in him not to pick up his office line and call his best bud. He kept watching the clock, trying to gage how long it would take for their meeting to end. He hadn't got much work done all afternoon, his mind was too focused elsewhere. He was anxious to know the outcome of Carlos's meeting. Reds had spoken to him that morning. As soon as his alarm clock went off he gave him a ring

….."Hey, hey man you ready to be a super star!" he shouted through the line in Carlos's ear no soon as he said hello.

"You ready to see your name up in lights man?!?" Carlos chuckled, still half asleep. Reds was giddy.

"Man listen, don't go in there talking a hole in his head. Listen more than you speak. What you wearin? . . . Suit up bro if you have to, so he can know you about your business, and another thing don't…"

"Hey hey, okay man, I got this alright." Carlos chuckled, cutting through his words. I appreciate the support black man, but I got this thing in the bag…*trust*!"

Reds sat at his office desk, chewing on the back of an ink pen, thinking about this morning's phone conversation. *"Damn I hope he got this!"* He said aloud. One of his colleagues was standing at the copier machine not far from his office door. He looked up from what he was doing thinking Reds was speaking to him.

"Who screwed up?" the guy asked.

"Huh?...nobody, I'm talking to myself." Just then Carlos rang his line.

He reached over his desk, shutting his office door. "Wassup man? Reds answered anxiously. Carlos beamed on the other end. *"Reds I got it, we signed an agreement, man I'm in!"*

"AAAAAAAAHH MY MAAAAAN INNNNNNN!!! MY MAN GOT OOOOOOON!!! Reds shouted excitedly....Aaaw man I KNEW you could do it!!!!...I *knew* you had it in you Los! Man I'm so proud of you, you just don't know maaaaan......*YESSSSSSSS!!!"*

"Thanks brah," Carlos said between laughs. Yeah it feels good, things are all good right about now. Look I called you first so let me go, I wanna call Tammy and give her the news."

"We gotsta celebrate man...We gotta toast this thing up!" Reds shouted cheerfully.

" Okay let me see what she wants to do, maybe we can all go out together? I'll see if she and Crystal wanna tag along?" Reds was excited. "That sounds like a plan maaaan"...allright, I'll wait to hear back. Man you just made my "YEEEEAR" with that news brah!....WooooWeeee... Oh hole' up....Can I be the first to get your autograph?"

Both men laughed heartily, before hanging up... without saying goodbye.

———————◆———————

Carlos gazed out the back of the car window. He treated himself to a rare cab ride home from the studio, skipping the train. He sat there letting it all sink in. Contemplating everything that had just taken place. He thought about his stint in jail, all those sleepless nights behind bars dreaming about this day. He felt a huge ball of pride begin to well up at the bottom of his throat. He fought back tears. He was grateful that he was in a cab and not on the train with a crowd of people around. He breathed heavily, blowing the heavy emotions out from his nose. "How can one man be so lucky?" he thought. He sat there, looking out the window at all the passing buildings, allowing the sweet smell of success to linger a little while longer....

———

Tammy sat in the empty styling chair beside Crystal's work station. She laughed at Amina who was showing them how she "drops it low" in the club. Amina's small frame was bent forward as she bounced up and down, her arms flailed all over the place. Pouting her lips she said, "yeah all yaal haters wish you were me." Tammy laughed so hard she almost fell out the chair. She kept leaning over the side of it, holding her chest yelling "stop it!" "Stop it Aminaaaaa!" Amina kept right on dancing. Crystal shook her head at her assistant, as she continued placing spiral rollers in her client's head, who was also laughing hysterically. Crystal and Amina were an item almost as long as the shop was in business. There was no one Crystal relied on more than her young assistant. Their relationship throughout the years flourished.

"Amina stop your madness and go check on the lady under the dryer!" Crystal tried hard to contain her own laughter.

"But Miss Cryss you should have seen me doing it like this," she said, still bouncing. Her eyes now rolling up to the back of her head.

"*If.... You.... Don't.... Get.... Up.... From.... That.... Floor..... You better!*"....Crystal said, grabbing the back of the salon chair for support before attempting to playfully kick her young assistant. Amina shifted her position trying to get out the way of her foot and toppled backwards, falling the short distance to the floor. All the women laughed at that, including Amina...

"Ya'al see how she be treatin me right?" She said as she scraped herself up off the floor. "Ima call social services on you!" Tammy laughed the hardest being aware that was an inside jokes. Every time she thought Crystal was being too hard on Amina, Tammy would come to her defense, "stop yelling at that girl like that before she calls SSA on you!" she'd say.

As Amina walked off to go check on the client, Tammy's cell phone rang. She knew it was Carlos from the ring tone she'd saved for him. Prince's voice blurted from the phone, *"might not know it now, baby I'm a staaar. I don't wanna stop, till I reach the top..."* Tammy froze, shooting a look of excitement mixed with fear over at Crystal.

"Take it in the break room," Crystal said to her, knowing full well what the look was all about. Tammy stood and walked towards the break room near the back of the salon.

"Hey Ceee-Los" Tammy answered, attempting to sound cheery. Not knowing if her cover was blown. She knew she'd have to come out soon to both men, but she wanted to give Carlos a chance to advance up the ladder first. She was confident if Tre knew about her and Carlos, he'd do everything in his power to sabotage the relationship. Including blowing his chances at a record deal.

"Heeeey Baby I got some good news" Carlos said. The excitement in his voice set her mind at ease, at least for now.

"What happened?" Tammy asked anxiously.

"I'm signed!" He proudly proclaimed. "He signed me to the label!"

"I'm so proud of you Carlos, I knew you had star power"...she added.

"Thank You" he said with confidence.

"Tell me all about it, where are you?" She asked. Carlos chuckled, I'm in a cab on the way back from the studio now. I'd love to tell you all about it over a celebratory toast...How bout it? You wanna come out tonight?

"Of course!!!" Tammy cheered. "Okay where's Cryss?" Carlos asked. "Reds wants to come along too, I think he's more excited about this thing than I am . . . I thought maybe we could make it a double?"

"Oooh that's a good idea!" Tammy exclaimed. I'm here at the shop with her now, hold on let me see what she says." Tammy short jogged it back towards the front of the salon. "Cryss, Carlos wants to celebrate tonight, he got signed with Tre! He wants you and Reds to join us for a toast later?"

"I don't know whether to jump for joy or stab myself in the chest," Crystal said rolling her eyes at Tammy. Tammy shushed her friend, using her free hand to cover the mouthpiece pressed up against her face.

"What time should I tell him?"

Crystal looked over at the clock on the wall. "Ima need another couple of hours before I wrap up here. I got two more heads and then I can cash out, but I can get Amina to do that for me. Tell em around eight thirty – nine o'clock."

"We can meet you guys around nine" Tammy said in the phone, walking back towards the break room.

"So this is it huh… Now you're a star?" Carlos laughed at that notion.

"I'm *your* star!" He added. "You know I couldn't have done this thing without you Tammy. You… *and Crystal* were instrumental in putting this thing together. I'm forever grateful.

"Awwww cut that out, your talent got you this far, not me." Tammy was grateful for someone in her life to share these moments with. There was no doubting her feelings for him. Their love grew stronger and stronger with each passing day.

"Are we meeting at the same spot?" she asked him.

"Same spot!" he replied.

CHAPTER 16

———◆———

REDS SAT AT THE BAR watching the Redskins play the Cowboys on the big screen when Carlos walked up behind him. He grabbed him playfully around the neck, placing him in a rough rousing choke hold.

"Yeah . . . who's the man now, huh??...huh?" Carlos growled in his ear. Reds stiffened his shoulders in a hunch, allowing his friend to rough him up.

"Maaaan you must feel like a million bucks!" Reds said through his wide grin as Carlos took a seat beside him. Reds ears were blood red from all the commotion.

"I do.. man *I do!*"

"Where's the ladies?" Reds asked, looking back toward the door.

"I dunno? They should be here soon though," he responded.

"What you want to drink? My treat...Whatever you want it's on me... You've earned this one brah." Carlos glanced up at all the bottles of liquor lining the shelves behind the bar.

"I can top shelf it?"

"Yep! Go head...top shelf it tonight!" Cause once this mula start rolling in, alllll the drinks gonna be on *you* after that!" Carlos tossed his head back, accepting a hearty laugh. He felt good.

"I guess you're right." He said adjusting his body more comfortably on the stool.

A young bartender walked over, both men noticing right away how attractive she was. Grabbing a damp rag from under the counter she began wiping the bar in front of them. She wore a low cut tee shirt with the name of the bar's logo on front. They watched her intently as her half exposed breasts moved with every stroke of her hand.

"What can I get you guys?" She said turning slightly to toss the rag over into a small sink behind her. She placed both hands on her curvy waist, knowing all too well the impact her figure had on them.

"Umph" Carlos mumbled to no one in particular. He glanced up at the rows of bottles behind her.

"Aaaaaah let me get a shot of Patron." They watched her from behind as she turned to reach for the bottle. Both men zeroing in on her back side. Her tee shirt rose up slightly exposing the tips of some blue laced panties underneath her tight spandex pants. Carlos tapped his friend's leg under the bar, just to be sure they were both enjoying the same view. Reds leaned in closer to Carlos, reading his mind... *"your girl's on her way, I aint got no girl!...."* Carlos raised his hands in surrender, giving Reds the signal she was all his without a fight. They turned towards the two chatter boxes coming up from behind.

"*YOU* said you had it before we even got in" Crystal scorned.

"I didn't say I had *CASH*," Tammy shot back at her as they made their way to the bar.

"What's wrong?" Carlos asked them.

"This one here suggested we take a cab, but *aint got no money to pay for it!*" Crystal said pointing a distressed finger at Tammy.

"I said I don't have any *CAAASH*," Tammy shot crystal back a look of frustration. The cab is out front and he's not taking cards. We just left *her* shop, she aint think to bring no cash with her either while she keep trying to blame *me!*"

"Never mind, I got it" Reds said getting up from his seat. "I'm surprised he let you both out his cab without paying first, if it was "*us*" the cops would be coming by now." He added, shaking his head in frustration as he went.

"Thank you Mister *Reds*" Crystal shouted to him as she began taking off her leather jacket and matching gloves. Carlos turned completely around on his stool, facing Tammy head on. He looked her up and down slowly, taking in her entire presence. He noticed everything from her pointy toe boots and deep blue jeans to her leather jacket with rhinestones around the elbows and shoulders. A chunky rhinestone studded ring popped out from one of her fingers. Tammy had just let Crystal color her curly locks a mahogany brown that morning, they now fell perfectly across her shoulders. Carlos was in love. His eyes locked with hers for a brief second before moving on to scan the rest of her.

"You changed your hair" He said in a low tone. Grabbing her gently around the waist, pulling her in until she was pressed up against his thighs. At that moment there was no one else in the room, in the *world*, but them.

"You like it?" She asked, tossing her head to one side, grinning slyly. "I like everything about you," he responded right before locking his fingers around her tiny waist and pulling her in close for a long sensual kiss.

"Eeew, get a room!" Crystal shrieked, snapping them out of their trance state.

It took them a few seconds longer to fully recover from the spell. Tammy turned and placed her back up against Carlos' chest, he gave her a tight squeeze around the belly, taking in a full whiff of her freshly manicured hair.

"You smell good baby" He said.

"*Shut your jealous self up*" Tammy spat playfully over at Crystal.

"Jealous of what? Two damn horny horns going at each other in a public bar?" noooo hun, I'm not jealous, I'm embarrassed!" They laughed at her.

"Congratulations Ceeeee Los," Crystal said sincerely. I can't wait till the album drops. Based off what I heard at the studio, I *know* its gonna be a hit!

"Thanks Crystal" he said reaching out and giving her a fist bump but still holding Tammy tightly around the waist. Reds walked up and took a seat beside Crystal at the bar. They began having light conversation, which gave Carlos and Tammy more time to engross themselves in each other.

"*I wanna taste you*" Carlos whispered softly in her ear. Tammy closed her eyes and allowed her head to fall back freely onto his chest.

"You hear me?" he said gently caressing her stomach. He glanced around to be sure he didn't have any onlookers before easing her shirt up over his hand. Her body muscles contracting to his touch. Trusting him completely in that moment, she allowed him to inch his fingers further up her shirt. He reach her bra before she decided to stop him. Turning to faced him she asked coyly, "What are you doing silly?"

"*Chill out baby, aint nobody looking*" he said. Reaching this time for her ass. "Ceeee…no….stoooop…." she wiggled, moving his hands as he tried to reposition them further down her pants. He knew he could've pressed it with little resistance. The sound of her voice told him she *really* didn't care for him to stop. But from the corner of his eye, he could see that the young bartender was watching them. He could've cared less who was watching really, but knowing Tammy would be uncomfortable with it, he let up.

"*Get off me then…you tease!*" He said, playfully forcing her up off him. She gave him a soft slap across the face.

"Did you eat?" She asked. Carlos looked down at her crotch and back up into her eyes.

"I told you what I wanna taste" he replied. She felt the heat of his words down her pants. She looked intensely at him before turning her attention back to the other two.

"Hey Reds," she cut into their conversation. "Gimme a hug, I haven't seen you in a while!"

"Yes… yes it has been a while he said pulling up from his stool to give Tammy a big bear hug. "What are we eating? I'm starving!" She said.

"Should we grab a table?" Crystal asked. They all agreed that was a good idea....

———————

Two hours and several drinks later, they found themselves in a stupor. Reds was telling funny "*back in the day*" stories about he and Carlos. The girls were tickled pink as they hung onto every word.

"Stop it Reds, he could've been *that bad?* Tammy suggested.

"Are you kidding me! Reds squeaked, the alcohol taking its toll on his voice.

"*This guy right here staaaaaayed in some stuff.* For him to not have been intoxicated for half his life, like the rest of us... he stayed in hot water!" Tammy glanced over at Carlos lovingly. She couldn't help but to notice the change in herself sense they began dating. She felt at ease around him, safe.

"So Los, when do you start recording?" Reds asked. Carlos took a swig of his ice water, aiming to bring his liquor high down some.

"Next week."

"You should make some time to come with me to the studio" Carlos said. Tapping Tammy's thigh under the table. Tammy and Crystal shot each other a look of horror.

"We'll see" Tammy responded, deliberately avoiding his eyes.

"What you mean *we'll see!* He said. I need you there, for inspiration. At least one of the days next week.

"I'm not sure, I gotta see my schedule" Tammy said, anxious for the conversation to switch.

"I'll come hang with you Cee Los, this time I won't say nothing," Crystal said giggling at herself. They were all over the legal limit, except for Tammy, she'd always been the responsible one. Tammy could sense where the conversation was headed, she tried steering it in another direction;

"How's house selling coming along these days Reds? Sold anything fancy lately?" But to no avail. The studio conversation simply held more weight around the table.

"Yeah, I've been meaning to ask you Crystal, why'd you keep cutting me off like that when we were there with Tre?"

"Ask your girlfriend!" Crystal blurted without thinking. Tammy was mortified! Completely caught off guard.

"Ask her what?" Carlos said looking confused. If Crystal's words weren't enough cause for damage, her eyes were more as they grew wide as saucers. She slapped both hands across her mouth as if shutting her own self up from saying anything more.

Carlos looked hard at Tammy.

"What is she talking about?" He asked in a stern voice. Tammy looked down at her clenched fists, the table grew quiet. Her mind was racing. She wasn't sure what to say. She contemplated covering up her story with another story, but could think of nothing. The silence grew deafening around the table.

"What is she talking about?" Carlos asked again. At that moment Tammy knew she had to come clean, Carlos was nobody's fool. She couldn't see herself slithering out of this one.

"Ummmm Tre doesn't know about us." She said finally, still looking down at her hands. Carlos thought for a second on what that meant. Confused he prodded for more information, the other two looking on intensely.

"What you mean? He doesn't know about what?" His eyebrows drawing closer together.

"He doesn't know about *us*, us two, my relationship with *you!*" Carlos looked over at Crystal, and then to Reds and back again at Tammy.

"What the hell that dude got to do with *us?* Carlos asked, starting to appear worried. Tammy grew silent again. She wasn't sure what to say. She wasn't sure if this was the right time and place? If it was proper to be discussing this in front of them? How he would react? She felt as if she'd just hopped onto an emotional roller coaster without a safety belt. More seconds of silence creeped by...

"Aww come on Tammy, you aint gonna do this to me... *what?*" Carlos said defensively. Tammy breathed a heavy sigh, looking directly into his eyes.

"If he knew about us, he probably wouldn't have given you the appointment to meet with him." Tammy felt a slight sense of relief come over her, like a burdensome weight had been lifted. He thought about what she'd said....

"Why not? He *like you* or something?" Pushing his body away from her as a mental puzzle began forming in his mind from the fragmented pieces she was offering.

"*Like her?...Tre is in looove with her!*" Crystal blurted out through her drunkenness. Tammy shot her a look that could've killed a mockingbird. She wanted to strangle her at that moment.

"He has this crush on me, but he'll get over it" Tammy said nonchalantly, trying desperately to diffuse the situation. She looked up at Carlos and was frightened by his expression. Carlos turned his attention across the table to Crystal, realizing he may be able to gain more answers from her.

"So Crystal, that's why you came and met me at the studio..huh?"

"Soooo that's why you kept cutting me off when I was talking to him, huh? So y'all think you're slick?" Finally Reds spoke up. He nudged Crystal's arm with his.

"I think we should go for a walk and give these two some space," His voice still squeaking from too many celebration shots of Patron.

"Nah, nah noooo man" Carlos said extending his arm across the table to stop them from moving. He had sobered up swiftly. Nah man let her stay right *here*!...She knows something about this too, I wanna know what the *hell's goin on?*" he said desperately.

"What the hell is she talkin about Tamm?" He demanded, growing frustrated.

"I just told you," Tammy said, "he has a crush on me!"

"So you're telling me that if he knew about us, our relationship, that I wouldn't have gotten this *record deal?*

"I don't know, probably... probably not, I'm not sure" she said, shrugging her shoulders. Crystal shook her head in disdain. "*Tammy don't do that*" she said between hiccups. "*Tell him the truth, it's all out in the open now.*" Crystal had an ulterior motive herself, she wanted to clear her own name. She had no intentions of letting this thing drag out any further than it already had.

"Okay okay" Tammy said, becoming irritated by the truth of it all, "he likes me… okay. But I don't like *him* like that." Throwing the last part in for good measure.

"He sabotaged a situation with me and someone else before, I didn't want to take any chances, so I didn't elaborate about us." He allowed her words to sink in. "So I wouldn't even have this *contract,* if he knew what was up…with us?" Tammy didn't answer. Carlos felt defeated. All his excitement, all the celebrating, all the laughter…gone. Feelings of hopelessness, fear and betrayal taking their place.

He stood up sharply, reaching down to grab his jacket off the seat. He began putting it on slowly without saying a word….

"Where are you going?" Tammy asked defensively. He didn't answer. He reached into his back pocket, pulling out his wallet. He grabbed two twenties and a ten from the billfold and let them fall to the table, then turned and walked away. Reds jumped up, grabbing his own jacket from the seat beside him. Not bothering to put it on he looked over at Tammy.

"I got this…okay. Give him some time," he said. He dropped a couple more twenties on top of Carlos', quickly jogging his way out the door to catch up with his friend.

PART TWO

CHAPTER 1

———◆———

ANYE WATCHED FROM HER FRONT door as her brother shut the yard gate behind him. Using one foot she held the screen door open to her tiny row house. Extending her arms wide to greet him. Carlos wrapped his arms around his sister's chunky waist like a life raft in a drowning ocean. They stood there locked in embrace for longer than a moment. Carlos wanted to cry, but was successful in blocking that notion. Instead, he allowed the comfort of his sister's embrace to relieve some of the stress he'd been harboring the last twenty-four hours. Anye understood her little brother better than anyone else on earth.

"Awwww Carlos I've missed you so so much," she said.

"Let me look at you!" Carlos lifted his head from her shoulder and allowed her to cup his face with her chubby hands.

"Look at you!" she smiled, studying his face.

"Come... come. Let's go inside." Taking his hand, she led him inside. Carlos hadn't seen the inside of his sister's home in more than four years. It was just as he'd remembered. The couch still had the same muddy brown upholstery he remembered, the television sat in the same corner, above it the shelves held the same wood carved figurines. The tall African men with long legs, holding wooden sticks in the shape of spears. The curtains were the same brown with floral print he remembered them to be. The only pop of color to be found in the entire room were the plastic yellow placemats displayed on the dining room table. They were spread out for no one in particular. They were more for show than substance. Looking around the place gave him a sense of belonging. He was comforted by the familiarity of it all.

"I wasn't able to sleep at all after hanging up from you last night," she said.

"Are you hungry?" I fixed breakfast...and lunch! Carlos chuckled at his sister. She reminded him of the description in Maya Angelou's poem "phenomenal woman" She was not cute or built to fit a fashion model's size, but she was phenomenal.

"I am starving ...What you got for a brother?" He said, slapping both hands together, rubbing them back and forth in anticipation. He followed her into the tiny kitchen where a pot covered every burner on the stove. She began peeling back the tops of each one by one, stirring the contents and calling off the names of each as she went.

"Here's some bean soup, and some scrambled eggs with cheese, and some turkey bacon over here, 'cause I know you don't eat no pork. You da one got me to stop eating pork, from that letter you wrote me, remember that? There's grits over here and some fried potatoes, I have biscuits in the oven."

"Got dang girl!" Carlos said cheerfully. "I know you aint cook all this for me??? Where da man at? Where he hiding?" He joked looking around as if he was searching for someone. Anye laughed...

"Naaaw aint no man up in here, I wish there were some nights, but naw no man." Here, help yourself, the plates are up there." She pointed to one of the wooden cabinets worn from age.

"Ima run down and get this last load of clothes, they should be done by now."

"You need some help?" Carlos asked her, reaching up to grab a plate from the cabinet.

"Naaah I got it" she replied, leaving him to fend for himself. She sat across the table from him folding clothes as they made small talk while he ate.

"So what *really* bought you down this way Cee?" "What happened?" She asked him. When they spoke the night before, he didn't offer any concrete explanations for his prompt visit. He told her he'd missed her and wanted to come pay her a visit. Of course she agreed, but knew him well enough to know there was more to the story then that.

Carlos pushed his finished plate to one side, placing both elbows on the table...

"Aww man sis, where do I begin?" He breathed a heavy sigh, scratching the back of his head where it didn't itch. Anye folded her hands in her lap, patiently waiting for the beans to spill.

"I met this girl right, awesome girl... but she lied to me."

"Lied about what?"

"She lied to this record producer, I've been talking to. Let me back up...I got a record deal." Anye's eyes grew wide..."*really!*" She was about to congratulate him when he put his hand up in a gesture to stop her.

"Wait before you go and get all worked up and excited, it may not be nothing, let me finish the story." Anye was confused, so she allowed him to continue.

"This girl I've been seeing, Tammy, the one I told you about before?" She shook her head in acknowledgement. "Well she's friends with this big time record producer, Tre.

"Tre?"

"The same Tre with Concrete Jungle?" she asked excitedly. That's the label you're signed to? She desperately wanted to celebrate his success.

"Yeah but hold on, hold on let me finish... What you know about him anyways?" Carlos asked.

"I keep up with that sorta stuff because of *you're* interest in the industry. I need to know what's goin on up there in that big city. I get the *Source* magazine. "It's around here somewhere she said, looking around in search of it. I just read an article about him a few months ago...he's tough!"

"Yeah well...that's him." Carlos said. "They're friends, he and Tammy are. From what I understand he aaah *likes* her or something." He couldn't bring himself to use the word love. "So I'm hearing if he finds out about us, me and Tammy, he probably won't be cutting this deal with me.

"Oh really!" Anye said angrily. "How did she lie?"

"See this is where it gets complicated . . . She told him I was dating her best friend, so he wouldn't suspect anything between the two of us, and now it's all fucked up." Anye though about what he'd shared.

"Does he know about it? Tre?" She asked.

"No! Crazy part is *I* wasn't even supposed to know! I don't know how they thought they'd keep this thing under wraps"…

"They? Who's they?" Anye was confused.

"Oh yeah, I forgot to add…Her friend Crystal was in on it too…She's the one who set up the meeting with me and Tre."

"Do you love this girl?" She asked him.

"Yeah… I do." It's why I'm so messed up in the head, I don't know what to do."

"Do you love her more than your music career?" She went straight for the juggler.

Carlos breathed heavy…he found himself angered by the question.

"See this is why I'm so pissed. Why do I have to *choose*? Why can't it be both?" She felt her little brother's pain. She'd never been in love before, but she could imagine what he was feeling.

"You can always go to another producer, can't you? I mean if he saw the talent in you, I'm sure there are other producers who would too?"

"You don't understand, this dude has the largest label *in* New York. He *runs* the hip-hop scene! All he gotta do is put out a few calls, aint nobody else gonna mess with me if he throws dirt on my name. Besides I already signed with him." Anye thought on it. She desperately wanted to fix his problem. Ever sense he was little she'd always come to his aid. She took a lot of rough beatings growing up saving him from harm's way. With no kids herself, he was as much her child as her brother.

"Gosh, this is a tangled mess" she said, rubbing the side of her face.

"What about Tammy? What happened there?" He sat slumped in his chair. His belly heavy from all the food he'd just eaten.

"Did they have a past relationship or something? Why is he so fixated on her?" She was still perplexed by it all.

"I asked her that. She told me they were just friends. Man this is crazy," Carlos said dropping his head and shaking it back and forth in disgust.

"What's your plan?" She asked him. Understanding full well moping was not gonna solve anything.

"I don't know yet, I fumbled around with all kinds of different scenarios the entire ride down. It's one reason why I wanted to come . . . to talk with you about it.

Carlos disregarded his probation officer and his boss. Deciding instead to hop on the first bus going down to D.C. that morning.

"What you think I should do sis?"

"I really can't be mad at her, she said. Sounds to me like she was trying to protect you."

"Carlos nodded in agreements."

"I still love her, he sighed. That aint gonna change. I mean, I'm mad 'cause she lied.... *Dissapointed* really. I aint never known her to lie like that." He thought about his own secret he was withholding, the one concerning his boss. At that moment he felt like a hypocrite.

"As long as she don't make a *habit* of lying to protect you. I think you should speak *candidly* to her about it. Set the tone *now*! That's if you plan to be with her after this. She must be special if a guy like Tre is so sensitive about her," she added.

"*She is.*" Carlos said without hesitation...."*She is.*"

"I don't know *what* to say about all this Carlos. It's one of those damned if you do, damned if you don't scenarios."

"Yeah, you're right"...he said painfully.

"I suggest you give it more thought. Maybe it'll all work itself out. Sleep on it. Sleep has a way of helping to clear the mind.

"Yeah, you're right."

"Use this free time to clear your head, and make some *thoughtful* decisions. But don't stress over it Ccc, it'll work itself out... it always docs."

CHAPTER 2

———————

TAMMY WAS A WRECK. SHE was not feeling up to climbing out of bed, but she had online work to complete. Her computer screen sat blank. She hadn't slept all night "again" from the occurring events over the last few days. She wanted to call Carlos to assure him she was sorry for the web she'd placed him in. But the fear of rejection prevented her from picking up the phone. Normally, they spoke everyday... sometimes two and three times a day, chatting about un-important things just to hear each other's laughter. She was now filled with fear and uncertainty about their future. She'd grown to care for Carlos deeply and missed him. She thought of Tre and grew angry. She resented the power he had over her. She thought about going to visit his studio and telling him straight up how she felt about Carlos and demand that he not come in between what they were building. But deep down she knew that would not go over well with him. She knew he'd only take his emotions out on Carlos, which was the very thing she was attempting to prevent. She'd really made a mess of things, and felt bad about it.

Her phone rang. A wave of emotion rushed over her thinking it could be Carlos calling. Only to go flat when she saw it was her dad. She thought about letting it go to voicemail so she could continue wallowing in her sorrow, but decided instead to answer. Tammy knew he'd only continue to call every hour on the hour until she picked-up.

"Hey daddy" She answered in the most cheerful voice she could muster.

"Hey Sweetie how you doing?" She didn't feel like giving a long drawn out explanation so she fabricated the truth.

"I'm doing okay, what's up?"

"Well aaah, I called to tell you, you have some more mail over here..." Tammy's heart sank even further.

"Mail from who?" Asking but knowing full well the answer.

"It's aaah... another postcard" her father said cautiously. Tammy grew quiet. She hadn't told a soul about the first one. She'd convinced herself it was an isolated incident and if her mother really wanted to connect with her, she would've given a return address. Tammy figured she'd be better off protecting herself from more pain by not getting attached to that part of her life.

"Is there a return address?" she asked him.

"aaah nooo it doesn't seem to be," he replied. Her resentment grew deeper.

"What does it say?" She asked, curiosity getting the best of her.

"Hold on let me get my reading glasses..." Sam came back to the phone a few seconds later... "Hello, you there?"

"I'm here"

"Okay aaah it says...

"I pray my messages are reaching her, if so, please give her this number 555...."

"Looks like she's trying to reach you Tamm." Tammy grew angry.

"It's been twenty-nine freakin years" she spat. "Fine time to try and reach me now!"

"Awww come on now Tammy, we don't know her side of things" he said.

"I can't *believe* you're taking up for her! SHE left ME! She left *YOU TOO!*"

"Yes yes...this is true," her father said softly, attempting to diffuse her anger with his voice. "I've forgiven her a long time ago for that... long time ago baby girl. It's not healthy to hang onto that kind of anger."

"Well, I'm not angry but I aint *happy-go-lucky* about it either!" He knew that wasn't the case. He knew exactly how she felt because he'd lived with those same emotions for years.

"I didn't call to get you upset sweetie" he said. Just know you have some mail over here if you want to come retrieve it."

"Okay... thanks. She said in a much softer tone than before. "I appreciate the call."

"Tammy! If you need to talk with someone about all this, please call me you hear?"

"Okay... I will" she responded half-heartedly.

"Love you baby girl."

"Love you too Dad." Tammy hung up and sat there looking at the flashing icon on her blank computer screen. She felt emotionally drained. Her thoughts went from Carlos to these random postcards. She played the recorded scenes over in her head of the moments from her past. Short scenes that involved her mother. She could only recall a few. Any remembrances of her mother's face were long gone from her memory bank, replaced in later years by a few photos and family discussions here and there. She recalled being around eight years old, staying one summer week at her cousin Mia's house in upstate New York. She didn't see that side of her family often as it was no hop and a skip from the city...But she remembered one particular visit vividly. The time when her aunt showed her the picture....The one with her Mother...

"Tammy come here chile and tell me who dis is?" Aunt Betty motioned for Tammy to put down the toy she'd been playing with and come to where the grown-ups had congregated. Her Aunt had company over. A group of ladies were sitting around with stacks of old photos and wine bottles spread over the table. Each of them were sifting through a stack, laughing loudly as they sipped from their glasses.

"Come er, look at this picture an tell me who dis is?" Tammy walked over taking the picture from her aunt Betty's hand. She noticed her father's face right away and quickly went to hand the picture back, "It's my daddy!"

"No chile, look again...who is that *wit* your daddy?" Tammy's innocent eyes took a second look, this time studying the face that stood next to him. Her father posed confidently in front of a wide tree. A boyish grin plastered on his face. The stranger stood beside him wearing a polyester dress that flared out at the waist, cutting off right below the knee. Her hair was tied neatly in a bun. Tammy remembered she held her purse with both hands out in the front of her, as if she was hiding... or protecting what was underneath. The lady had skin the color of rich chocolate. She looked sad. Tammy's young eyes tried to figure out who the woman was but had no recollection. Finally, shrugging her shoulders she handed the picture back to her aunt.

"I dunno? She'd grown bored with the game, anxious to get back to her toys.

"That's your *mother* chile!" Aunt Betty shouted with a chuckle. The others around the table joining in on the amusement.

"Damn shame dis chile don't even know her own mother's face." Betty said taking the picture from her little hands and placing it back on the pile with all the rest.

"Go on chile, go on and play" she said shooing her away.

Tammy never forgot that. She could recall a few other memories from her childhood where her mother was mentioned, but that time, at her Aunt Betty's, held the deepest memory for her. Those words forever haunted her,

Damn shame dis chile don't even know her own mother's face."

She thought back to what her father said. That she shouldn't be so angry. Tammy *was* angry. She didn't like revisiting those old tattered feelings of abandonment. She hid those feelings *behind* the anger. Eventually, she'd grown sick of hearing about her mother, she wanted nothing to do with her. She thought if she could erase the image of her mother from her mind all together, she wouldn't have to feel the pain. She knew her dad and Nana were sincerely trying to help by sharing memorable moments, but it had gotten to a point where any time she heard the words, "your mother," sharp pangs went through her chest.

She wanted those pangs to stop. So once, when she was in her early teens, they were all in the car together returning from one of her dance recitals. She, her Nana and Sam. Her father pointing out the window at a park as he drove past it. "Look over there...see that park!" he pointed, looking back at Tammy with excitement to see if she were witnessing it too. "That there's the park your mother used to bring you to when you were just a little girl." He went on to elaborate... "she used to take you on the swings and..."

"Look can y'all quit it with all the "*your mother*" stories!" She said, cutting into his words harshly. "I don't wanna hear all that...it just makes me mad." He and Nana gave each other a concerned look. After that incident, they never mentioned her to Tammy again. She figured some time later that they must've had a discussion about it, when she wasn't around. Deciding together it was best if they granted her wishes....

Tammy's focus came back to the blank computer screen in front of her. The tiny clock in the corner of the screen read 9:47AM. She'd been sitting there over an hour and hadn't begun a stitch of work. Her heavy thoughts dragged back to Carlos. She sighed and punched down on the keyboard harder than necessary. Closing her eyes she said a brief prayer, asking for the tide to turn.

CHAPTER 3

TRE HELD THE DOOR OPEN so the young girl who was with him could walk through first. Once inside he walked swiftly ahead of her, fully expecting she would follow.

"Aye Mike!" he shouted loudly, listening for a response. "Yo Mike!" he called again as he made his way to the back of the club. It was an early weekday morning, the place sat eerily still compared to the hustle and bustle of the night life he was accustomed to witnessing in the place.

"Yo Yo, I'm back here man" Mike said poking his head out from one of the small rooms in the rear. Mike barely greeted them as they reached the room, he was preoccupied with some forms he held in his hands.

"Yo what's the urgency man?" Tre asked walking into his office as Mike walked over and took a seat behind his desk. He looked up for the first time and noticed the young lady standing in the doorway, looking uncomfortable.

"Who's that?" Mike asked him, a little irritated. Tre turned to look at the young lady he was with, and for a fleeting moment he couldn't recall her name. The thought of this embarrassed him. Playing it off, he nodded in Mike's direction.

"Tell em who you are" he said to her. She looked like a frightened young child who was totally out of her element, hunching her shoulders over and giving Mike a terrified look.

"I'm Angel" she said shyly. Mike looked over at Tre, scolding him with his eyes.

"Angel, Tre and I need to talk about some important business, would you mind waiting for him out in the car?" Angel was relieved by this news. She wanted nothing more in life at that moment than to separate herself from the cold stares and sympathetic attention.

"Okay" she managed to say. But stood there like a child waiting for further instructions.

Tre looked back at her, growing irritated himself by her severe timidness.

"Go head, tell my driver I'll be out in a few" he said, not bothering to escort her back out the door. Mike waited until the clapping sound of her heels against the concrete floor grew faint before speaking.

"What are you doing man? That girl looks like she could be your daughter!"

Tre chuckled. "She's old enough…trust me… I checked her I.D. last night before I let her in the ride." Mike gave him an even more disgusted look than before.

"You need to slow your road, for real man." He said shaking his head. "You gonna find yourself in more shit than necessary."

Tre knew he was right. But didn't come there to elaborate on his sex life.

"What's up?" Tre asked, ignoring his remark all together. "What's the urgent matter?"

"You need to settle down and find a wife, all jokes aside man." Mike decided to give his point one last push before laying it to rest.

"Well, until Tammy is ready to marry me, I gotta take 'em as they come." Tre laughed at his own words, attempting to lighten the mood in the room, but Mike was not amused. He just shook his head in disgust, directing his attention back to the papers in his hand.

"We got a problem." Remember that dude, the balloon man I referred you to for your accounting?"

"Yeah, what about him?' Tre asked as he walked over to the chairs stacked up in the corner of the room, pulling one off from the top of the pile.

"He's in jail."

"IN JAIL!" Tre shouted... holding the chair suspended in mid-air as he searched Mike's face for an explanation.

"Yeah man, and it don't look good." He extended the papers out to Tre so he could read them himself. Tre sat the chair down taking the papers from his hand.

"This is a summons!" he said after reading a few lines.

"Awww come on maaaan," Tre said slamming himself down hard in the chair, beginning to understand clearly what this meant for them both.

"Did you get anything in the mail?" Mike asked him.

"No...not that I know of. Barb didn't mention anything to me. When did you get this?" Tre asked him.

"Yesterday."

"Damn! I had a feeling that dude was gonna be trouble, I should've listened to my first instinct...*Damn it!*" Tre balled the corner of the paper up in his fist out of anger.

"I'm sorry man," Mike told him under his breath. "I never saw this coming. I've been working with him for years. And even prior to that, he came highly recommended from another club owner who'd been working with him for *at least* a decade before me. I didn't see this coming at all man." Tre didn't respond. He continued reading the paper. Mike sat there waiting, holding a hand against his head...

After reading it thoroughly, Tre took the paper and slung it across the table, landing it near Mike's propped elbow.

"This is big Mike. This could set us both back big time man."

"Don't remind me." Is all Mike could bring himself to say. Tre reached inside his suit jacket for his phone. Using his thumb, he scrolled up a few times before punching a familiar number. He waited for Barbara's voice to greet him on the other end.

"Concrete Jungle!" she sang cheerfully.

"Hey Barb it's me...Listen did I get any mail recently from the court house? It would've come from..." Tre sat up in his chair and began searching Mike's desk with his eyes. Mike knew he was looking for the envelope the court paper came in, but he threw it away that morning. He grabbed the paper up from the desk that Tre tossed and pointed to the top of it before handing it back across the desk to him.

"It would've come from New York County, Manhattan`division court house?"

Tre held his breath...

"Nooo I don't think so boss," she said. "But let me double check."

Tre waited impatiently as he heard her flipping through papers on the other end.

"I just looked through the mail I have here on my desk again, I don't see...oh wait a minute....yes here's something...its from the courthouse."

"*Shit!* Tre stammered"

"She hesitated before asking, "is everything alright sir?" Barbara worked for Tre long enough to recognize his mood swings. She knew when it was okay to joke with him, to give him his space, or be concerned enough to ask delving questions. Something in his voice gave her cause for concern.

"Everything's fine Barb... just leave it on my desk before you leave alright?" he told her. Barbara hesitated a second longer, deciding against probing any further, she told him she would.

Tre put the phone back in his pocket and focused his attention on the floor. He thought hard on what to do next. Mike's voice cut into his thoughts.

"Maybe the bulk of the mess skipped us altogether. Maybe they aint got nothing at all on us. All this may be standard procedure or some shit?"

"How did they get *your* information?" Tre asked, looking up from the floor.

"From what I understand, his place was raided."

"Raided!" Tre said in surprise.

"Yeah....not good huh?" Tre breathed a heavy sigh, sitting up in the chair. "We work too hard to be taking these kinda risks man".... Mike nodded in agreements.

"You got a good attorney?" Tre asked him. It was Mike's turn to breathe a heavy sigh.

"To be honest, I haven't even thought that far ahead. I spent half of yesterday worrying about my business and the other half worrying about yours."

"Well, don't." Tre said. "I knew what was up from the get go. I made the decision to allow that nutcase to handle my accounting. I made that choice, not you. So don't feel bad. But you should start looking for a good attorney though bro. This dragon is not gonna go away on its own, we're gonna have to fight it."

"I'll start requiring on my end too, just in case," Tre said. We may be able to save some on the bill if we got a shark who'll handle both our cases, as one."

"Yeah I know, I know man. I'm just hoping we won't take a huge fall from all of this," Mike said.

"So do I man...so do I!"

CHAPTER 4

———————

CRYSTAL SAT QUIETLY ON THE passenger's side as Reds finished up his phone call.

"Both offers on your home came in lower than the list price" He was telling a client on the other end.

"Yes, but keep in mind Mister Brown, that against my better judgment, we priced your home above market value when we initially placed it up for sale. Coupled with it being listed for more than a month now, two offers slightly below list price is great news!"

Crystal began studying her fingers for something to do to pass the time. She noticed her nails were chipped and uneven. She made a mental note to visit the nail salon on her next day off. She noticed she had color on one finger where red hair dye had seeped through a hole in her glove at work. Seeing the stain reminded her of earlier days when she would put fruit punch flavored cool-aid in her hair to color it. She chuckled to herself at the thought of how far she'd come.

Reds gave her a raised eyebrow thinking she was laughing at something he'd said. She shook her head and waived her hand at him as if to say 'never mind me.'

"I'll have time tomorrow to come over and present you both offers. We'll discuss then what recourse of action to take. I'm here with the most beautiful woman in the city, and she's been extremely patient with me up to this point, but I don't wanna disappoint her by spending all my time here on the phone chatting it up with you sir!" Their eyes locked, Crystal gave him a warm smile of appreciation.

"No no...no problem Mister Brown, he continued, you couldn't have known, but I appreciate your understanding," Reds said into the phone. "I have some time in the early afternoon tomorrow, I can come by then?...okay great...perfect...see you then.

They were parked at the corner of one of Crystal's favorite places to eat, Seasoned Vegan in Harlem. The restaurant was always jammed tight with people, today was no different. Neither of them were vegan, but Crystal liked to eat there every chance she got for a healthy spin on a good meal. They sat in the front seat of Reds car he used mainly for taking clients out to show houses. He shifted his body weight in the drivers seat of the small sports car so that he was facing her.

"Thanks for being so patient with me" He said.

"Oh I understand it honey...when duty calls...it calls!" she snapped her finger in the air to drive home the point. Reds grabbed her hand, pulling it closer to him.

"What's this" he asked, looking at her finger concerned.

"Oh that's just hair dye" she said nonchalantly.

"Someone left your shop looking like a parrot today?" Crystal laughed at him.

"How does it taste?" Reds asked her, still examining her fingers.

"How does *what* taste?" she was confused with his question.

"This dye?" He took her stained finger and gently placed it into his mouth, caressing it back and forth using his tongue. Crystal was surprised by this move. She'd been hanging out with him more so than usual these days and was beginning to see another side of him she hadn't noticed before, a softer, more romantic side. She enjoyed his company, but they never went past first base. They kissed a few times, soft pecks, but nothing more than that. She wanted to stop him, to pull her fingers away, but something prevented her from doing it.

"What are you doing?" She asked in a sensual tone.

Ignoring her he began using the same technique on her other fingers. Once he'd tasted every one of em, he released them back to her. Crystal didn't know how to respond. It felt good, but not good enough to pursue things any further. She looked to see if the dye stain was still there. Sure enough, it was right where it was before. A little moist to the touch, but there.

"How did it taste?" she asked jokingly.

"I'm not finished yet" he said as he reached for her other hand. Crystal moved it from his grasp.

"I'm not letting you lick all over me in this car" she said sassily. Reds laughed.

"Alright, fair enough...he said" Reds had selfish thoughts running through his head. Crystal knew exactly where his head was at. She decided she'd keep quiet and allow him to play his hustle game on the long trek across town. The whole ride he kept schmoozing her ego with fluffy compliments and soothing words. As they pulled up to the front of her building he let the car idle. Reds gave her a surprised look..."aren't you gonna invite me up?" he asked. Crystal was not one for holding her tongue.

"Come up for what?" she demanded. Reds chuckled, using the sly grin that worked so well on other women in this same predicament"

"Come on Cryss...stop playing, ima park the car and come up for a lil while."

"For what?" she asked him again.

"What you mean *for what*, you know...I'm tryin to be next to you." Crystal was not amused. She looked straight into his eyes, more intensely than before. She responded in her usual blunt fiery way.

"Let me ask you something" she said. "What's my middle name?" She didn't bother waiting for a reply before shooting out another question...

"When's my birthday?" "What's my *HIV* status?"

"You don't know a personal thing about me, *for real*, but you wanna get *next* to me?"

Reds tried thinking of a clever response but could come up with nothing.

"Good night Reds... thanks for dinner."...She dismissed him by exiting the car. He took his scarred ego with him along for the ride as he headed home.

CHAPTER 5

———◆———

CARLOS SPENT THE ENTIRE MORNING and half the afternoon maneuvering furniture nonstop. Even though the weather called for a jacket, he'd worked up a serious sweat without one. He grinded like a madman straight through his lunch break. He feared if he took up too much idle time, his thoughts would revert back to Tammy or Concrete Jungle . . . A week had passed sense he'd last seen or spoken with Tammy. He missed her profusely. Over a million and one times he picked up the phone to dial her number, only to hang up before the call went through. These were new feelings for him. He'd never felt this way before about a woman. Not having total control over his emotions, made him feel weak.

Tammy reached out to him the morning after he returned from D.C. He answered her call long enough to tell her that he needed some space. She pleaded with him to let her come over so they could talk more about it in person, but Carlos refused. The tone of his voice warned her that he meant what he said, so Tammy reluctantly agreed to his demand. But Carlos was now wondering if teaching her a lesson was more torture on himself than on her. He was a wrecking ball of nerves.

"Aye yo Los...somebody here to see you man!" his coworker Lance shouted at him over the music blasting from the radio in the loading dock. This news froze Carlos in his tracks. No one ever came to his job looking for him. The legs to the table he was packing onto the truck were poking out from the top of the pile of furniture.

"Who...*me?*"

112

"Yeah *you!*" Lance shot back …some chick…a cutie… She asked for you. She's in Ms. Neffie's office now." Carlos's heart stopped! He knew it could only be one person, and the fact that she was in his boss's office sent a wave of fear down his spine. He moved quickly, so fast that one of the legs he was stuffing came tumbling down and hit the truck's bed with a bang, he didn't even bother picking it up. He moved briskly towards his boss's office, peeling his work gloves off and wiping the sweat from his brow as he went.

"How long she been in there?" he asked Lance as he passed him.

"Hell if I know, what's up wit you man?" Lance asked frowning.

"She been in there long?"

"I don't know . . . Boss lady just told me to come get you…*What's wrong?*" He curved the corner and stopped right at the entrance of her office door. Tammy's back was turned away so she didn't see him. She stood over Ms Neffie's desk, her jacket still on. The pink scarf he'd gotten her as a gift draped around her neck. Carlos could tell from where he stood that she was holding something fragile in her hands.

Ms. Neffie was sitting behind her desk, looking up at Tammy. She was saying something to Tammy and stopped in mid-sentence when she saw Carlos at the door. "Tammy!" Carlos called her name cautiously. Uncertain of what his boss had said to her. She didn't turn to look at him. Her shoulders were hunched stiffly as if she'd just been frightened by a large animal. He knew by her body language; Ms Neffie had spilled the beans. "Tammy!" He said her name again with more force, shooting his boss a look filled with venom. He walked up behind her, reaching out for her shoulder. She felt his hand and hunched away from him like a frightened child. She never said a word. He could see the pain in her eyes. Her beautiful brown eyes were filled with so much pain that they almost bought tears to his own.

"Tammy please listen" he said mercifully. She sat the container she was holding onto the desk and backed away from him like he was poisonous. Stepping backwards until she reached the door. She then turned and walked away. He noticed it was a container of food she'd left behind.

A bag lunch for him he surmised. In that moment Carlos felt defeated. He didn't have the energy to go after her. He sagged his head towards the floor. His neck muscles stretched so tensely you could see his veins.

Turning his attention to the enemy in his midst, he let out a furious roar... *WHAT THE FUCK DID YOU SAY TO HER*!!!! Carlos slung the work gloves he was holding in her face with all his might. This reaction took Ms. Neffie by surprise. She stood up swiftly, catching her eye glasses as they fell off her face.

"I told her the truth!" Ms. Neffie shouted back in freight. Carlos felt every vertebrae in the back of his neck snap one by one. He'd reached the max of his stress level, the tea kettle had come to full steam.

"What the fuck did you say to her!!!" he shouted through clenched teeth, making his way around the desk toward his prey.

"Los!" Just then Lance rushed in, grabbing him from behind right before his hands reached her neck. He forced Carlos's hands back down to his sides.

"Calm down man, calm the hell down!" Lance shouted in his ear, squeezing him tightly around the chest. He began dragging Carlos back, away from Ms. Neffie. Both men were a match, pound for pound so it wasn't difficult for Lance to maneuver him.

"I quit this fuckin piss hole...you hear me old lady . . . I QUIT!" Carlos shouted... nose flared. "Take this job and shove it you fuckin freak!" "I quit!"

"No! No! Los...you don't mean that..."

"He don't mean that Ms. Neffie, Lance tried pleading on his behalf.

"Oh yes the hell I do....I'm done here man. Let me go!" He said struggling to get out of Lance's grip. The two ladies who worked the customer service desk heard all the commotion and came running back to see what was happening. Lance let him go, he quickly maneuvered in front of Carlos, acting as a buffer between them.

"You're gonna pay for this shit" Carlos said, pointed a stiff finger over Lance's shoulder. "You watch you old hag...you gonna pay!"

Ms. Neffie looked like a deer caught in headlights.

"Washed up old hag!" was his last words before storming out of the office. The ladies who were posted up by the door moving swiftly out his way. Carlos went back into the bay area and began retrieving his personal belongings. Lance walked up as he was gathering the last of his things.

"Hey Los, I'm not sure about what just happened in there, but you may wanna rethink the idea of quitting." Carlos was uninterested.

"That's right Lance, you don't *know* the half . . . so I suggest you stay out of it!" he said, the anger still simmering in his blood. Lance liked Carlos, they were buddies. Lance was the site manager for the warehouse. Out of all the employees on payroll, Lance preferred to work with Carlos above any of 'em. Carlos was a hard worker who rarely missed days, someone who pulled his own weight AND SOME OTHERS, Lance could spar with him, an all-around decent guy. Lance knew it'd take *three* men to replace the value Carlos single-handedly bought to the place. He tried pleading with him again...

"Carlos you're on probation man, you and I both know how hard it is to get a decent job while on probation."

"Well maybe that's just it" Carlos shot. "Maybe I don't *need* no damn job!"

What are you saying?" Lance asked in surprise. "We all need our jobs." Won't you just take today to calm your nerves . . . take a breather and we'll talk about it tomorrow? Okay...I'll call you in the morning alright?" Lance said, a hint of desperation in his voice.

Carlos placed the last of his things in his duffle bag, zipping it shut. He turned and looked Lance square in the eye.

"I appreciate you Lance, but I'm done here. I mean it...I'm not interested in no more jobs...I'm done faking. Ima use this gift I got if it's the last thing I do.

"It was nice knowing you brah." Carlos slung the backpack over his shoulder and headed out the door...

CHAPTER 6

TAMMY LEFT THE WAREHOUSE AND headed straight to her Grandmother's home. She needed a safe haven, someplace she could go and comfort her soul. When she showed up un-announced at her door, Nana knew instantly something was terribly wrong with her grandchild. Tammy's normal fun loving spirit had all but left her body completely. She looked the same way she felt, as if something inside her died. Nana took one look at her and worry implanted itself in the wrinkles on her face.

"Nana he's cheating on meeeeee" was all Tammy could utter before the pain of it all came rushing to her lungs.

"Awwww Baby...come here...come here child," Nana said, stretching her arms out and wrapping them across Tammy's body. She walked Tammy into the living room, to the velvet rocking chair in the corner. One assisting the other as if neither was able to walk on their own. Nana sat down and pulled Tammy across her lap as if she were a toddler again. Tammy lay her head against her grandmother's shoulder. There they sat rocking, back and forth in the red velvet rocking chair. Tammy crying like a baby in her grandmother's arms. Nana stroked Tammy's curly locks as she rocked. Tammy tried talking through her tears, *but why Na ough Na? Whyyyyyy meeeee.*" Her grandmother hushing her. "Shhhhhh shh shh shh chile.... Don't talk...she said...just listen, listen to your soul chile. Listen!" Finally after ten minutes of silence, Tammy stood and wiped her wet face with her hands. She took a seat across from her on the couch. Nana continued to rock.

"I found out today that Carlos was having sex with his boss, this whole time." Tammy told her, cutting straight to the chase. Nana didn't appear surprised. After eight decades on earth, she'd seen her share of heart breaks.

"Who told you that?" Her grandmother asked firmly.

"She did! His boss did! Tammy responded defensively.

"Why did she say this to you?" Nana asked her. Tammy thought about the question. Her grandmother was a wise woman. She had a very keen sense of seeing "through" situations. Tammy guessed this time was no different.

"I don't know why she told me," Tammy said. Not wanting to think too deeply about it, preferring instead to just wallow in her shallow pain.

"Yes you do know why," her grandmother prodded. Now tell me…. Why did that lady tell you this?" Tammy decided to focus more intently on her question.

"I guess she wanted to hurt my feelings." Tammy said.

"Do you know this woman?" Nana asked her.

"No!"

"She is a stranger to you?" Nana said, to drive her point home.

"Yes!"

"Now why would a complete stranger want to hurt your feelings?" Nana said, with a hint of sarcasm.

"Why did she tell you this?" Nana asked her again.

"None of that matters!" Tammy said growing frustrated. What matters is that *he* lied to me! He did not tell me he was having *sex* with her! It's *him* I blame…not her!"

"Have you spoken with him?" Nana asked.

"No!"…And I have no plans to either" Tammy said.

"Aren't you interested in the truth?" Nana asked her. "How do you expect to gain the whole truth if you don't speak with him?"

"What kind of explanation could he *ever* give me," she said through her pain, "to make it alright?" He can't tell me *anything*, I don't want to hear it.

117

"I didn't suggest you excuse his behavior, I said speak to him so that you can gain the whole truth, for yourself. With truth comes clarity darling, it is best if you seek clarity in all things. Life becomes easier to bear when you have clarity." Tammy thought about those words carefully.

"I don't think we can get past this Nana."

"Then don't!" she told her... Tammy sighed heavily, deciding to change the subject to another matter that was weighing heavily on her.

"Did daddy tell you about the postcards?"

"Yes, I'm aware" Nana said....Still rocking.

"What do you think I should do?" Tammy asked her. Nana stopped rocking for the first time since she sat down. She leaned up and looked Tammy square in the eye...and said....

"Seek the truth child!"

CHAPTER 7

———◆———

IT WAS CARLOS'S FIRST OFFICIAL day in the studio. He decided since he and Tammy weren't communicating, it wasn't even necessary to mention her to Tre. Tre had asked in casual conversation how Crystal was doing and he decided to just go along. Carlos told him she was doing fine and left it at that. They began laying the first track for the album.

"You got some serious talent young blood!" Tre told him, "a little more refining and you'll be a solid hit." Carlos was grateful Tre had confidence in him. He needed his confidence more than anything else at that moment. He didn't mention he'd quit his job either. He figured the less Tre knew about his personal life, the better off their work relationship would be. Carlos was finding it a challenge to remain focused with the headphones on. Hearing his own voice resounding back in his ears seemed foreign to him. He kept trying to take them off, but every time he did, Tre would reprimanding him.

"Keep em on man, get used to having them ON! After several times of Carlos snatching them off his ear Tre lost patience with him...

"Look man... I'm tired of saying it... keep em ON!!! You're making this harder on the both of us. Just follow my advice or go home!" Tre was tough. He was fair, but tough on all his protégés. He simply had no patience for half stepping. Anyone working with Tre figured out quick they'd better be prepared to put some work in....or else. You may have walked into his studio a glimmer of hope, but you walked out a star! His track record spoke for itself.

119

"Let's do it again from the top. This time I need you to focus in on that third verse," Tre said. When you get there you're slowing down, watch out for that. Keep steady your pace all the way through. Keep the focus on your words, not your ears." Tre spoke through the mic.

"Leave the head phones alone! They're there to help, get used to 'em."

Carlos took a deep breath and listened for the intro. It wasn't a beat he would've chosen for himself, but the more he heard it, the more it grew on him. He had just as much confidence in Tre's ability to make fresh beats as Tre had in his rap skills.

Carlos was a storyteller. He vowed that if he ever got this opportunity, he'd stay true to his roots. He made a commitment to the art form. He refused to be just another sell out rap artist who got by with recording foul nursery rhymes over dope beats, he wanted nothing to do with that. He knew his fans deserved more than that. Everything Carlos wrote about had a deeper meaning, a back story. He was grateful it was Tre he was working with. Out of all the other labels, he knew Concrete Jungle would be the most faithful to his art form.

He began again… *No love for a homie in the heart of the city, where words are gritty n dogs aint pretty….*

"Alright man…sounds good sounds good in there" Tre said when he was done. Now this time I want you to add a sig." Carlos was confused. "What's a sig?" Tre forgot for a moment he was dealing with a first-timer.

"A *signature piece*. A tagline that lets people know who you are without you telling em." Carlos was still perplexed.

"When you think of DMX… what sound comes to mind?" Tre asked him.

"grrrrrrrrrr" Carlos growled.

"Exactly! Dog man!" When you think of Mike, what comes to mind?" "Heee-heee" Carlos said, raising up on his tippy toes.

"Right! That's a sig! Now what's yours?" Carlos thought about it. He didn't have a sig but he was excited by the idea. He could think of nothing.

"I tell you what" Tre said, sensing he was stuck. "I want you to really get into this next set. I mean feel it. Don't think about the bridge, don't think about the plosive, the cans, nothing… just spit… from your gut. When you feel it, in that moment, just let it out! Whatever that "it" is, it doesn't need a name…Whatever you spit out…that'll be your sig…okay, got it?"

"Got it!" Carlos replied. Feeling up for the challenge. Tre started the beat up again… This Time Carlos squeezed his eyes shut. He blocked everything out around him, focusing in on the beat. He allowed the percussions to flow through his veins, engrossing himself in sound. The words came gushing out of him like a waterfall. He reached the second verse and that's when something hit him. "bouiee yaaah" he said. He didn't stop to analyze this newfound sound before rushing head first into the third verse. Flowing beautifully all the way to the end. As the beat made its outro, Tre's voice burst through the headphones…

"That's it!" "That's it young blood, we're finished . . . NOTHING needs changing!" Carlos smiled from ear to ear. He came out and took a chair beside Tre at the sound booth. Tre played the song back on the loud speaker so they both could listen.

"We got a hit on our hands right here young blood….I can feel it!"

"*Sho nuff*???" Carlos asked excitedly.

"Listen, I know a hit when I hear one. *This is a hit!* Tre said,…still bobbing his head forcefully… *this is a hit!* Tre took his earphones off and hit the mute button. He turned to give Carlos his undivided.

"Okay one down…nine more to go" he told him. "At this rate we may be done sooner than I thought." Ima set you up with a few key folks so they can begin slotting us in their calendars. You're gonna need a media coach and a choreographer. I'll give my baby a call to see if she has room for you…I'll be…." Tre went on to say something else but Carlos heard nothing after that…Those words "my baby" was all he could focus on.

"Who's the choreographer?" Carlos asked him, cutting him off in mid-sentence.

"Tammy." your girl Crystal's best friend. "You know her right?" "I'm sure you do, those two are inseparable." Carlos was crushed. His heart went down to his stomach. He thought about those words again "*my baby*" and felt sick. He shot Tre a look filled with venom, he slid his chair back away from him with his feet.

"You alright?" Tre asked in surprise. Carlos realized what he was doing, and turned his head away in embarrassment.

"You alright?" Tre asked him again.

"I'm good" Carlos said sternly. He sat there while Tre finished running down the list of things they needed to prepare for, but he may as well've been speaking Russian, Carlos heard nothing else.

CHAPTER 8

———◆———

CARLOS LEFT THE STUDIO AND headed for Tammy's house. Having to sit in that studio and listen to Tre describe her as "his baby" was more than Carlos could handle. He could not wait another day, he had to settle the unrested emotions in his body. He knew her daily routine, and knew she'd be reaching home from the studio at any second. He knew she'd be running bath water soon, her nightly ritual. He hadn't seen or heard from Tammy since the incident at the warehouse a few days prior. He wanted to reach out to her sooner but thought better of it. He figured giving her some well-deserved time and space would help to clear the smog filled air between them. But the time lapse was beginning to feel like suffocation. He didn't bother calling, he figured he'd gain better results if he showed up in person.

He tapping lightly on her condo door. Sure enough, Tammy was in the bathroom running water in the tub. It wasn't until she'd shut the faucet off that she heard the light tapping. "Tap-tap-tap-tap"... a sound she could barely make out. She wasn't expecting visitors so she dismissed the sound as coming from her neighbor's door. She began removing her clothes. She placed them in a neat pile on top of the toilet. She went to dip her toe in the water and heard it again...This time louder than before..."tap-tap-tap-tap." There was no doubt that the sound was coming from her door... Frustrated, she reached for her robe hanging on the back of the bathroom door. She slipped on her fuzzy pink slippers to go and investigate.

"Who is it?" she shouted in an irritated tone long before reaching the door.

Carlos said nothing. She looked through the peep hole, ready to dismiss whoever it was. Carlos's baseball cap obscured his face. Tammy could barely make out the silhouette in the dimly lit hallway, but she'd recognize that body anyplace, even in the pitch dark. Her heart skipped two beats. They both stood there stiffly, in their perspective places as the seconds passed, nothing separating them but a door.

"Who is it?" Tammy asked again softly, breaking the silence.

Carlos lifted his head so that his face was totally recognizable through the tiny peep hole.

"It's me… Tamm…open the door…I need to talk to you." He spoke softly yet confidently.

For a moment Tammy didn't know what to do. She wished Crystal was there to help guide her through this moment. Crystal was always better than her at filtering through these type of situations. Crystal was quick on her feet; whereas, Tammy seemed to need more time to sort things through. She leaned her forehead on the door next to the peep hole. Not sure how to respond, she heard his voice again this time low and even.

"Tammy open the door, I won't be long, I promise, I just need to speak to you."

Tammy's mind was insisting that she tell him to go away, but her heart pulled her in a different direction. As she stood there half naked, eyes closed, forehead up against the cold door, Nana's words came to mind. "Seek answers child!" Figuring this was a better time than none, and an excuse to go with her heart she flipped the knob that unlocked the door and let him in. Carlos walked past her through the door as she shut it behind him. She turned to face him and their eyes met. She looked so beautiful to him standing there in her thick white robe, her hair tied in a messy bun at the top of her head. He wanted to grab her and squeeze her tight but knew that wouldn't be the smartest of moves.

Instead he took her in with his eyes. She walked over and took a seat at the edge of the couch and waited for him to join her. He took a seat beside her. They sat there together, in silence for a few moments before he began…

"Tammy I miss you. I know I hurt you." She sat there without a response, looking down at her furry pink slippers. He continued…

"I didn't come here to make excuses for myself or try and convince you to see things my way, I just needed to see you. Tammy please look at me." She looked over into his eyes.

"I am dying inside Tamm…I miss you…I…."

"Why didn't you tell me about your boss?" She cut him off, her face growing harsh. Carlos took a long hard breath before answering. "I didn't know *how!*"

"I trusted you Carlos!" her voice cracking. He went to place his arms around her and she pushed them away…

"No!" was all she said before bursting into tears.

Carlos moved off the couch down onto his knees in front of her, a gesture of total submission.

"Tammy please….pleeeeease understand me…. I hated that woman!" His words came rushing out as if there were an hourglass nearby half filled with sand. "I quit my job Tammy, I only did what I did so I could keep my job. I hated her Tammy. I love you! Baby I'm sorry… please understand I don't want anyone but you! I can't sleep thinking about you every night Tammy please, let me make it up to you pleeeeease." His words were all jumbled together. They came rushing out like a burst dam. Nothing like he had planned. He reached up and touched her knee, still crying she moved his hand away.

Carlos felt tears begin to well up in his own eyes. He was deeply troubled knowing her hurt came from his doing. He thought for a second about what his boys behind bars would think if they saw him like this, down on his knees, near tears, pleading for a woman's affection. But he didn't care. His only concern at that moment was fighting for the love of his life.

"Tell me what to do Tammy??? I'm sorry...please...just tell me what to do, whatever it is I'll do it." She stood up and walked back over to the door, putting space between him and her feelings.

"Everything we had was a lie!" she spat. "I trusted you with my *soul* Carlos, and you disrespected that. You hurt me!" Carlos dropped his head in shame. He felt helpless. He knew he was hearing the truth. He had nothing left but his deep love to prove her wrong.

"You're right, he said. I have no excuses for what I did" He looked up at her pleadingly, "I tried to stop it several times but she kept threatening my job. I felt trapped."

"Trapped!" Tammy spat in disgust. "TRAPPED!!!" she repeated... driving the point home.

"I mean...I could have quit a long time ago yes... but then what would I have done for money? You don't want somebody who can't take care of himself... *or you*!"

"So let me get this straight" she said sarcastically, wiping a tear from her cheek and folding her arms across her chest in defiance. "You decided to fuck your boss for money?!"

"No" he said quickly, that's not what I....

"So help me understand then?" she said. Carlos thought about it. "We weren't together, you and I... when it started...I mean...I did it thinking it would help me get favor around the job"

"What kind of *favor?*" She asked digging for those answers her Nana suggested.

"I dunno...anything...for favoritism." Carlos was uncomfortable with the subject.

"So you used her?" She asked him.

"She was *using* me too Tam! It was wrong, I get that."

"Is it *now* wrong because I found out?" she asked. If I had never showed up at your job...would it still be *wrong* Carlos? When were you gonna decide it was *wrong* enough to put an end to it?"

"Tammy"... he stood up and tried pleading with her again but she stopped him by shaking her head.

"No Carlos, I heard you. There is nothing more to be said." She unlocked the door and held it open for him. Carlos was crushed. He wanted to demand that she shut the door, insist that she listen to him. But knew it was of no use. Tammy was a woman of integrity and he wouldn't dare try and force her hand. He knew that would be emotional suicide. He reached the door and stopped. ..."*You can't make me stop loving you*" he whispered near her ear right before walking out the door...

CHAPTER 9

———

"GIRL LET'S BLOW THIS JOINT, I'm tired of folks rolling their eyes at me" Crystal whispered.

"If you would quit talking…you could get into what they are saying. Tammy whispered back.

"They're singing too damn much for me. I aint know this was gonna be no musical." Tammy bust out laughing for the tenth time sense the play began. She covered her mouth but it was too late, the laughter beat her hand to it. The couple sitting right in front of them both turned around in unison, giving Tammy a stern look of disapproval.

"Okay…okay let's go," Tammy said nudging her friend playfully. As they got up to leave, Tammy couldn't help but to think of how grateful she was to have Crystal in her life. She was a good friend to her and always seemed to know just what she needed, when she needed it. They were opposites in almost every way, but their friendship had a common thread that withstood the test of time.

"I'm starving anyways" Crystal said once they reached the exit doors of the theatre box. "Let's go get something bad for us to eat. Aint nobody got time for all that singing and stuff, they play too much in that play!" Tammy laughed some more…

"Girl you're a mess! If we didn't leave when we did, they was gonna put us out anyways." Tammy reached out and locked elbows with her friend. They walked down the corridor of the playhouse arm and arm laughing hysterically. Once outside they walked down Broadway, checking out the outdoor menus at all the eateries as they passed them. They settled on a place called Bravo Pizzeria. Figuring the name would make up for the not so bravo feeling they got from the place they just left.

Crystal ordered a huge slice of extra cheese pizza while Tammy went the more conservative route. She settled for a Greek salad with a side order of plain breadsticks.

"You're so boring," Crystal said as they sat down in the back of the restaurant to enjoy their meals.

"What?" Tammy said surprised. She'd been smiling ever sense she and Crystal got together that morning. It was a refreshing break from a strenuous week.

"Look at you...why couldn't you be bad with me, just this one time?" Crystal said pointing over at Tammy's salad. You aint even get no *salad dressing.*

"I am being bad!" Tammy said. "Look... I got the breadsticks?"

Crystal rolled her eyes. Well you go right ahead, ima enjoy my heaping load of cheese. Ima pay for it later I know, but Ima enjoy this here block of cheese while it lasts."

Both ladies laughed at that.

"So tell me how you feel?" Crystal asked her in between bites.

"About what?" Tammy wasn't sure what she meant.

"About the whole Carlos thing?" Crystal was never one to beat around the bush. She had this uncanny knack of cutting through all the subtle pleasantries and getting straight to the point. She was the same way in all her dealings. If you didn't know her well, her straightforwardness could easily be mistaken for rudeness. But Tammy was accustomed to her frankness. Crystal had a good heart, she was just a straight shooter.

"Weeelllll" Tammy said giving her brain some time to mull over the question. She finished chewing before she added...

"I *do* miss him. I would be lying to myself if I said I didn't."

"Have you spoken with him?" Crystal delved deeper.

"No"

"Did he make any attempts to reach out to you?" Crystal asked.

"Not sense he popped up at my door the other week."

"Hmmm" Crystal said before taking another bite of her pizza.

"Is it over?" She asked.

"Aaaaah *yeah!*" Tammy responded, frowning her nose up at her friend, "What kind of question is that?" Crystal took a sip of lemonade from her straw before adding...

"You know Tamm, I like Carlos. I think you should give him another chance."

Tammy laughed before realizing Crystal was being serious.

"Eeeew Crystal, why would you say that?"

"I don't think you're looking at the bigger picture Tammy." She said. "Carlos is not the typical stiff suit guy you're used to dating. I think subconsciously, you want him to be though."

"*Whaaat!*" Tammy said in surprise, laying her fork down. "Where did *that* come from?"

"Just...just hear me out. So you say he was screwing his boss right?" Crystal went on without waiting for the answer. "And she was an old battleax right? And he quit his job after you found out, right? So this tells me that he was *only* doing it for the job sake. Clearly if he quit the dern *job*, he values the relationship he has with you over even his financial stability....And that's big for a man Tammy. Real big! And you and I both know Carlos aint no slouch, so for him to *quit*, that says a lot about how he feels about you."

"I can't believe my ears!" Tammy said, folding her arms across her chest. The salad in front of her now all but forgotten.

"Are you suggesting that I should just *ignore* the fact that he cheated on me?" Just so he can turn around and do it again down the line?"

"No I didn't say that" Crystal said defensively. I said you're not looking at the *bigger* picture. You are placing Carlos, the man who spent time in jail, the man who finds it hard to get a job, the man who did not have the same advantages as you growing up, the man who has no one to lean on for support . . . in the same category as other men you've dated. All I'm saying is you can't do that. His choices are based on *survival*, Tamm, not simple pleasures." Crystal took another bite of her pizza, allowing what she said to sink in Tammy's head before continuing.

"Now I'm not suggesting what he did was *right,* she said through chews. I'm just saying look at the *bigger* picture." Tammy thought about the last time she saw him. How he kept reiterating that he hated his boss. She thought about how upset he was at the lady for spilling the beans. She picked her plastic fork back up and began tossing lettuce back and forth on the Styrofoam platter.

"Last I checked, *you* haven't been completely honest within the relationship yourself Mary Poppins" Crystal said, using her tongue to drive the knife into Tammy's open wound.

"Yeah, but I kept that a secret trying to protect *him*" Tammy said, attempting to defend herself.

Crystal shot right back…"How is what he did any different?"

Tammy thought on it…"I dunno Cryss…That's kind of a stretch don't you think?"

"Is it?" Crystal said popping the last bit of pizza in her mouth and wiping her greasy hands off with a napkin. Tammy didn't respond.

"Well anyways . . . How's your dad doing? She asked, skipping the subject on purpose. Crystal was very clever, and she knew her friend well. She knew when to push and when to let go. She knew she'd said enough on the subject.

"He's good" Tammy said, allowing her previous words to sink in. The two women sat in silence for a bit, Crystal began looking around the pizzeria, focusing her attention on all the comers and goers while Tammy finished up her salad.

"Guess what else?" Tammy said after awhile.

"What else?" Crystal asked, focusing her attention back on the conversation.

"I received two postcards from my mother."

"What mother?" Crystal asked frowning her face up in confusion.

"My *biological* mother!"

"You're shittin me!" Crystal said. Her eyes growing big as saucers…"*When?*"

"I got one about two months ago, and another one came last week." Crystal's big surprised eyes turned to disappointment. "And you're *just* telling me about this?"

"I didn't tell *anyone*. I'm still trying to process it all myself."

"Where does she live?"

"According to the postcard stamp in Africa."

"I *knew* she went back home!" Crystal said, excited to be piecing the puzzle together. "It was the only thing that ever made sense."

"Yeah…my Dad had always thought she went back home too."

"What did the postcards say?"

"One just pretty much confirmed she was alive and the last one gave a phone number where she could be reached."

"Did you call her?"

"No."

"Why not?" Crystal asked her. "I don't get you" she said shaking her head at Tammy.

"So what's the plan? Crystal asked…We going on a trip to the motherland?"

"Pump your brakes" Tammy said, holding her hand out in front of Crystal as if to stop her. "I said I got two *postcards*…nothing more."

"What the heck you mean nothing more!? Crystal said growing frustrated with her friend.

"Don't you *wanna* meet your mom?

"I dunno…Tammy shrugged her shoulders. She should've thought about all this when I was three years old." Crystal gave Tammy a cold hard stare.

"Tammy you need to let go of all that malice girl. You don't know what your mother was going through all this time. Hell, from the stories you've told me, sounds like she wasn't happy here even *before* you came along. She's probably been suffering all this time… What mother can walk away from her child and not suffer because of it? You shouldn't be like that Tamm!"

"See...this is why I aint wanna tell you nothing" Tammy said growing angry. "I'm sick of everybody taking *her* side. What about me and my feelings? Huh? So my feelings don't mean shit, huh?" Tammy shoved the plate of withered salad away from her in disgust, letting her spine hit the back of the chair harder than necessary. Crystal didn't respond. She figured it would be best to just allow her friend's hot head to cool off some.

She grabbed the plate Tammy shoved away and pulled it in closer to her. She took her clean fork she never used for her pizza and began eating the salad. Tammy looked over at her and rolled her eyes..."You're so greedy!"

"Waste not want not" Crystal said through chews.

"What did Nana say about it?" Crystal asked after a few moments of silence had passed. Tammy sat there with her legs crossed at the ankles, shaking her feet antsy back and forth. "She told me to seek answers." Crystal didn't say another word...she knew she didn't have to.

CHAPTER 10

———◆———

CARLOS WALKED THROUGH THE DOOR of the Y looking around in search of Reds. It really wasn't his usual thing, but he figured since he had more time than money these days, he'd be better off making use of the time. He stopped briefly to flash the buddy membership card Reds gave him to the guy sitting at the front desk. He didn't see Reds anywhere in sight so he shifted his jean duffle bag from one shoulder over to the other and started for the rear where the basketball court was located. He knew if there were any place to find him, the court would be it. Sure enough, he walked in to find Reds playing a round of one on one with a tall, heavy set man. They must've been playing a while as both men were sweating profusely. Carlos placed two fingers in his mouth, whistling to get Reds attention "phee-eeet." Reds was completely focused on a dunk he was right in the middle of making.

"Boooyah two points…in your face!" Reds shouted, antagonizing his opponent as he landed skillfully on his feet. Reds clearly appearing to be the more athletic of the two.

Carlos whistled again, this time a little louder as he began walking towards the locker room.

"*I see you finally made it!*" Reds shouted out of breath, excited to see his friend.

"Ima change up!" Carlos shouted back, pointing over his shoulder at his bag as he made his way into the locker room. Carlos emerged wearing gray sweat shorts that cut off right below his knees and a white tee shirt. He wore his old beat up gym shoes that he used to wear to work, back when he still had a job.

"Wanna go another round?" Carlos asked Reds who was giving the heavy set guy some dap after crushing him on the score.

"Man are you kidding me… I'm tapped out!" Reds said, reaching for his sweat rag lying on the bleachers nearby.

"What took you so long anyways? I thought you said you'd be here like an hour ago?" Reds asked, wiping his face and head with the towel.

"I know, I got caught up at the studio longer than I anticipated."

"Oh yeah!" Reds said excitedly, slapping Carlos in the chest with the rag before wiping at his face again.

"How's that coming along?"

"It's coming…man it's coming" A lot more work than I thought going in. Which aint a problem for me, it's just I didn't realize so much went into making records.

"Hit Records!" Reds corrected him.

"It has a lot to do with Tre though, he's a perfectionist! I aint never worked this hard on my craft."

"Yeeeeah Boooooooyz, that means its gonna be a *hit*! Reds said, slapping him with the towel again, this time on his upper arm."

"Quit that shit fool!" Carlos said, allowing himself to get swept up in Reds excitement. He took a playful shadow box jab at Reds' face, missing his nose by half an inch.

"Come on, let's hit the weights" Carlos suggested.

"Yeah cuz you gon need to pump that squawny chest to flex for all dem chicks once this album drops!" Reds said jokingly. Carlos's face grew tight at the mention of that. He thought about Tammy. He didn't care about all the loose chicks. He was well aware of the type of groupie girls the industry attracted. Those type were of no interest to Carlos…at all. They could line 'em all up in a row a mile long… fancy, sexy, body like goddesses, erotic, and he would *still* choose Tammy over each and every one of 'em. Tammy gave him a taste of true love, what a high quality woman was made of. It made him almost sick to his stomach to think he'd never feel that again.

"How much longer you got in the studio?" Reds burst into his thoughts as they entered the weight room. There were four others there ahead of them, getting their work outs in. They both headed for the one available weight bench in the room.

"We can take turns" Carlos said. "I'll go first to give your no skill having ass time to catch your breath." Reds laughed as he walked around to the end of the weight pole to add an extra bar on.

"You talkin all this shit...Ima see what you gon be talking after these weights hit your chest." Reds began adding another fifty pounds to the already fifty that was there. Carlos noticed how much he was adding.

"Hole up, what you doin??? Naaaw man, take that off I aint even warmed up yet!"

"And *"I"* aint got no skills you say? You's a softy man. You mean you can't lift a hundred pounds?"

"I aint say I can't, I said lemme warm up first!" Carlos nudged Reds, moving him out the way as he removed the extra weight he'd added.

"Ima do a set at fifty, *then* I'll work my way up! I aint gonna let you talk me into pulling a muscle. *You* come here all the time, I don't!" Carlos said, explaining himself for his ego's sake. Reds chuckled as he shook his head, folding his arms he stepped to the side to watch his friend.

"What were you saying?" Carlos asked him. Reds thought back...

"Oh I was asking how much longer you gonna be in the studio?

"We got ten tracks to lay, we finished three. I aint sure? I told you that dude's a perfectionist" he said grabbing the poles to begin his set.

"He'll go over one track like a thousand times. I can hear it and think it's all good, but Tre be finding the smallest imperfections and I wind up having to do the track all over again. Shit's crazy man." He said between clenched teeth as he began his set. He completed thirty five, his arms could take no more. He stood up to allow Reds his turn. Showing

Carlos up, he reached down and moved the pin, placing the extra fifty pounds onto the weight pole.

"Lemme school you on how it's done." He said. Halfway through Red's set Carlos's cell phone buzzed from inside his pocket. He reached down to check who it was and was taken totally off guard. He immediately shot through the door of the weight room and headed into the empty lobby, to give himself some privacy.

"Hello!" He answered nervously on the third ring.

"Hey Carlos" Tammy responded, more nervous than he.

"Wassup girl I thought I'd never hear from you again" He said as he chuckled. Tammy didn't respond to that.

"How have you been?" she asked.

"I've been...alright. He said. "And you?"

"The same"

"What are you doing?" She asked him.

"Aaaaah me and Reds are over here at the Y getting our work out on"

"Mmmm, When you start working out?"

"Well I gotta do something constructive with my time these days, sense I can't spend it with you." He replied.

"What do you have planned when you leave there?" She asked, ignoring that last remark. Carlos's heart raced. He knew where this conversation was leading and he was excited about it.

"Nothing...why?" He responded without hesitation.

"I'd like to talk with you... in person... if that's alright?"

"Tonight?" Carlos asked her for clarification sake.

"I mean if you have other plans...."

"Oh noooo no no I don't, I can come over now if you want?" Not even caring that he sounded vulnerable. She hesitated a few seconds before responding.

"Okay...I'll be up until like ten" she told him.

"I'll see you in a few then."

Carlos hit the end button on his phone, all while checking the time. It read 7:49PM. He stood there weighing his options. He'd been out all day and knew he needed a shower. He could get Reds to drive him home and then hop on the train from there, but that would mean he'd be losing precious time. Tammy lived about five train stops from the Y. He thought about it some more. He concluded he'd take a quick shower there in the locker room, and put back on the same clothes he had on earlier. It wasn't an ideal plan. He'd much rather look his best when he saw her, but weighing the options, he chose saving time over face.

He walked right past the weight room not wanting to spare a second as he made his way to the locker room where his duffle bag was stashed. He figured he'd mention to Reds the change of plans on his way out the door.

———

After he'd quickly showered and re-dressed he walked back to the weight room where he found Reds on the leg curl machine. He watched Carlos cross the door. "Where you been and *where you going?*" he asked, giving him a once over look of confusion.

"I gotta go. That was Tammy calling; she wants to see me."

"Tammy!" Reds said in surprise.

"Yeah man" Carlos chuckled, still giddy. She just called out the blue and said she wanted to meet with me tonight. She wants to talk.

"Awww hell, I can't compete with *"that!"* Reds said, using his legs to start the motion up again on the machine.

"What you just took a shower?" Reds asked him, noticing the light reflecting off his still damp hair.

"Yeah maaaan" Carlos used his hand as a make shift brush, sweeping it across his head. "Had to freshen up…just in case…you know?"

"Yeah I knows how it be" Reds said laughing.

"That's bold of her to call you, I wonder what she wants to talk to you about" Reds thought aloud.

"I don't know, but the fact she wants to see me is enough for me. Let me get going before it gets late. Sorry to bail out on you brah, what can I say…

"Say no more! I feel you completely. Hit me up tomorrow to let me know how things went."

"Bet!" Carlos flipped his duffle bag over his shoulder, turned and headed for the door.

CHAPTER 11

———◆———

Tammy checked the grandfather clock hanging from her wall as she went to answer the door. The clock was a gift from her grandmother. One she'd inherited from her own mother. A family heirloom. It read 8:29.

"That was quick" she said as she closed the door behind him, following him over to the couch. She wore a long yellow silky nightdress and matching robe. She too had freshened up for the evening.

"Yeah I decided to make my way over right after I hung up from you, before it got too late."

"I appreciate that" she said softly.

Carlos sat in the exact spot he occupied the last time he was there. More than a month ago. He thought about the last encounter and scooted himself over an inch, just in case the superstition gods were looming. Tammy sat down beside him, turning her perfectly shaped body in his direction. She folded her feet up under her legs and grabbed the throw pillow that was propped up behind her, placing it on her lap more as a buffer than for any other reason. Carlos got a very good look at her for. He scanned her body from head to toe, slowly taking in her beauty. He missed her tremendously. He was grateful to be able to see with his eyes again the visions he put to memory.

"You look beautiful" he told her sincerely. Tammy blushed. She too had missed the way he looked at her and his ever flowing compliments, something no woman ever grows tired of.

"Thanks" was all she said. Carlos wanted to touch her badly. He wanted to lay his hand on her leg, he wanted to rub his fingers through her hair, to kiss her cheek.... something... anything! His skin crawled to be next to hers, but he wouldn't dare...Not at that moment, not without her permission.

"So what do you want to talk to me about?" he asked rubbing both his thighs in a back and forth motion, out of a desperate need for self-control. Tammy looked away, giving herself a brief moment to gather her thought. She breathed a heavy sigh and decided to just speak whatever came to mind.

"I miss you Carlos." Freezing in his tracks he said nothing...allowing her to continue.

"I've been thinking about all that happened between us. The situation with Tre, which I admit was not the most honest thing to do. And your situation with your boss... which was *really* not the most honest thing to do! I've been thinking a lot about it and . . . and I've been wondering... if there is anything left for us to salvage?" She looked into his eyes, with intensity. Carlos could see pain in them. He felt those familiar pangs of regret coming on but this time they were mixed with excitement. He loved her more at that moment than any other.

"Are you finished?" He asked her kindly. She nodded her head yes.

"Do you remember what I told you the last time I was here? What was the last thing that I said to you Tammy right there at that door? Do you remember?" She lowered her gaze as she gently stroked the pillow.

"You said I couldn't make you stop loving me." Carlos looked down at her lips, they aroused him. He leaned into her closer, whispering near her ear.... "Say it again!"

Tammy's mouth curled up into a soft smile. *"Say it again!"* he demanded.

"You'd never stop loving me" She repeated. He looked from her lips up into her eyes. They hung out there, both of them, for what seemed like forever. Neither one speaking, locked in a hazy gaze.

"Tammy." He finally broke the silence, speaking gently. "I need you to feel me, I mean really *feel* me on this... "*I have never in my life felt for another woman the way I feel for you!*" This time away from you has been hell for me. I need you in my life. I don't just want you, I need you!*"

Her panties grew moist from the sincerity in his words. She felt like a captured slave to her emotions. She too had never felt more for another man, but she didn't share this, fear held her back from speaking it.

"But I'm scared" she told him honestly.

"Scared of what?" he said frowning, pulling his head back away from hers.

"Of you! You... hurting me again." She dropped her head again, fondling with the fringes on the pillow.

"I never saw that coming Carlos. Do you know how I felt standing in that woman's office???....listening to her tell me in detail the things she did with you!" He watched as she winced, turning her head away from him in disgust. His heart bled out right there on the couch. Carlos knew he had damage control to do. But she was worth every moment of it. He thought about what route to take and decided to get out of his head and stick with his heart.

"It kills me that I put you in this position Tam. I've beat myself up a thousand times over it." His voice clearly weakened by her emotions. "I quit my job Tam, I've given all that up..."

"Why'd you do that anyways?" she asked, cutting into his emotions. "With her....why were you having sex with that lady if you didn't want to?" Carlos sighed heavily, dropping his head in shame. He sat back on the couch looking away from her. He focused in on a gold colored painting of Queen Nefertiti she had hanging from the wall. He thought about how to respond. After a few moments he spoke...

"You know Tammy, I never really gave it enough thought to figure it all out myself.... I believe in the beginning, when it first happened.... I felt kinda important... As twisted as that may sound it's the truth. I mean... I was never *attracted* to her. I think I used her to feel like I was the big dog around the place…or something. Like the owner chose me so I must've had some type of clout."

He grew quiet and thought about his own words before continuing… "I thought I could somehow *benefit* from the situation, use it to my advantage." Carlos felt guilty and ashamed at the same time. He shook his head, disgusted with himself. He went on…"And then after a while…. she started becoming possessive, you know?" He looked over at her and then swiftly back at the portrait. "I tried to stop it several times, even before you came along, I tried to stop it but then she started threatening me . . . my job. So I thought what the hell, and I kept at it…because I needed my job." He thought about that, allowing his words to sink back into his own mind. "And then when you came along… It got worse for me because now the guilt set in. "I fought with that lady *every day* Tammy…I swear I wanted to end it long before you came into my life. And then once we grew closer, you and I . . . I knew I had to keep my job to maintain some type of stability, not just for me, but in order to keep *you*… So then it all became a tangled web. I never meant to hurt you Tammy . . . *I swear*!" He looked at her,

"And that's the God honest truth." "I swear!" Tammy thought about what he'd just shared. In an odd way she hurt for the both of them. She even felt sorry for Ms. Neffie. The fact that she had to stoop to such levels for intimacy. She thought about what her Nana told her, about seeking answers. She understood clearly at that moment why that was so important to do….To seek clarity. She thought about Crystal. How she was the reason why he was even sitting there on her couch.

"I promise you this" He broke into her thoughts. "If you take me back you will never have to worry about another woman in *life* coming between us. You have my word!"

"In life!' Tammy contemplated those two words…"*In life*"….What was he saying?

"Well you're about to be a mega star in a minute," She said sarcastically. "It's gonna be a lot more *younger* versions of Ms. Neffies hanging around soon."

"I aint trippin off that" he dismissed her last comment with a wave of his hand. "I'm trippin off *you!*" he said, searching her eyes for a ray of hope.

Tammy grew quiet. She knew before he arrived that she'd be accepting him back into her life. The pain of being without him was far greater than the pain he had caused her. Little was he aware that she needed him just as much as he needed her. They both were in love... heavily.... deeply. The type of love that doesn't extinguish easily.

"What are you thinking?" He asked.

"I'm thinking about all that you've just said. I'm wondering if it's worth it to move forward."

"Worth it!" He said in surprise.

"Yes *worth it* Carlos! You can't just mosey in here and give me a sob story and expect me to just accept it all without question, without contemplation!" Carlos sensed what she was doing, he decided to play along.

"Okay...okay...I'm sorry...you're right" he said. Bringing his tone down a notch.

"I tell you what....what if we did this...we walked slow....What if we decided to go back to *pre*-relationship status? for now huh? Until you're more comfortable with...with us. How's that sound?" He didn't want to push her back over the edge, but he was determined not to leave there in the same condition that he came. Tammy thought about it, a bit disappointed.

"I'm not saying I'd be comfortable with you going out with other dudes." Throwing that in for added assurance. "But we can walk slowly for now, until you tell me that you're comfortable with picking up where we left off. What you think? Do we have a deal?" He extending his hand for her to shake it. She hesitated for a second before placing her hand in his. Instead of shaking it, he pulled the back of it up to his lips for a soft kiss.

"Now, he said. "There's just one more order of business we must tend to..."

"What?"

"Tre!"

CHAPTER 12

SHERRIE STUMBLED OUT OF THE doctor's office like the town wino. Wobbling back and forth barely able to stand.

"Aye...aye....you alright miss?" a stranger walking past stopped and quickly motioned to assist her in maintaining her balance.

"You okay?" He asked again, fully expecting her to topple over at any second. Sherrie could barely speak. Her eyes appeared detached from her soul, her hair was in disarray. Her snug tee shirt wet under the arms from sweat...She was a wreck!

"Yeeeeah, I'm good" she responded groggily...

"You sure mama?" He asked again...Looking her up and down, unconvinced. He couldn't help but notice how attractive she was, despite her shaggy appearance.

"Yeeeeah...yeah...I'm fine...." she said, arching her back to stand a little taller, holding her own balance to prove it.

The stranger hesitated a minute before moving on. He kept looking back as he walked, to be certain she was still standing. Sherrie closed her eyes and leaned against the cool brick of the building. She wiped the wet bangs from her forehead as the spring breeze swept across her face. Not knowing what else to do she stood there, eyes closed, with her hand against her forehead. A million thoughts ran through her mind. She held the paper the doctor gave her. Looking down at it again through hazy eyes. She tried reading the scribbled words written in red ink on the blue prescription paper, but it was difficult to see through the haze of worry and regret. She didn't know whether to cry, scream or laugh hysterically…. Blinking her eyes tightly she tried reading the prescription again…

Truvada 96 mg 60 tablets. One per day. With food.

Sherrie read the scribble over and over again, her entire past flashing before her eyes. Still numb, she pushed up from her leaning position on the clinic wall and began stumbling towards the street. She reached the end of the curb before collapsing her full weight to the ground.

CHAPTER 13

———◆———

BARBARA KNEW THINGS WERE PRETTY serious when she called upstairs to let Tre know his *attorney* was here.

"Okay, let him up" was all he said to her before hanging up.

"Okay sir, you're fine to go up but I'll need you to sign here please and state the law firm you're affiliated with in parenthesis." She made him sign the visitor's log, knowing full well that wasn't necessary. She'd figured since Tre wasn't offering up any information; she'd do her own investigating. As soon as the elevator closed behind him, Barbara pulled the sign in sheet down from the top of the desk and read what he had written. She punched google up on the computer screen in front of her and typed in the hand written content.

Tre was wrapping up a session with one of his artists when the attorney walked through the door. The first thing Tre noticed was that he wasn't carrying anything with him. Saying nothing about it, he walked over to greet him. He was a very tall, slim figured man who looked more like an ex basketball player than an attorney. Tre shook his hand firmly and escorted him to the lounge couch that doubled as the waiting area.

"Thanks for coming on such short notice" Tre said to him. "Gimme like five minutes and I'll be right with you. I'm wrapping up a live session now."

"Sure, sure, no problem the attorney said politely. He'd never been to a studio before, so he was delighted by the opportunity to be able to sit and watch. He noticed there were three other guys in the room. Two very large men who looked like bouncers were over near the windows. One was looking down at the people below while the other guy sat beside him on the floor watching the third guy in the booth.

"Okay this'll be the last set Flo...then we'll wrap this up for the evening."

The young guy in a Yankees cap gave Tre a thumbs up signal from the sound booth.

"I'm turning your speakers down two notches, this should help with your high pitch," Tre said as he fondled with a few of the rows and rows of knobs that were sprawled out on the board in front of him. Flo shook his head in acknowledgement and then placed both hands over his earphones, preparing to take in the sound coming from them. Once the music started, he began rapping to the beat and the attorney's eyes grew wide as saucers.

"That's Flo Charts!" He said in amazement to Tre as if he was sharing some news with him he hadn't known. Tre ignored him, fully engrossed in his craft. He was busy flipping switches and turning knobs, adding different elements of sound to the beat while Flo carried on with the magic from the booth.

The attorney sat there smiling widely. He couldn't believe he was watching the same young guy he'd heard over the radio hundreds of times before. He made a mental note to call his nineteen year old daughter from the car. She was a huge fan of his.

Once the music came to an end, the large guy wobbled his way up from the floor, grateful no doubt it seemed that it was time for them to leave.

Flo took the headphones off and stepped out of the booth. Walking over to Tre's work area he nodded in the direction of the attorney acknowledging him before diverting his attention back over to Tre.

"How was that?" He asked him.

"Not bad...not bad" Tre responded. We still gotta work on getting the percussion to match your rhythm, but it's coming along. I'll work on some new sounds over the weekend and have em by next session. Get outta here and stay away from them clubs. I don't need to read nothing else about your social life in the paper, you feel me?"

Flo chuckled...yeah man I feel you." He gave Tre some dap and he and the two rhino's that were with him headed for the door. Tre turned a few more knobs on his machine and then focused all his attention on the attorney who was still sitting there grinning from ear to ear.

"Mr. Williams it is correct?" Tre asked.

"It's Bobby Williams, but just call me Bo... Everyone calls me Bo"

"Alright...Bo!" Tre said. Standing and walking towards his office. We can come and sit at the desk, I'd assume you need to write down some things? Tre's said looking down at his hands, addressing with his eyes the fact that he was empty handed.

"Oh I never work in paper form on the initial consultation," Bo said as he stood up to follow Tre into his office. "It's distracting. All I need is this"...He reached into his back pocket and produced a small voice recorder, holding it up so Tre could see it.

"A tape recorded huh?" Tre asked...a bit surprised.

"Yep!" I do have your permission to record this session correct?" Bo asked him as if he was fully expecting a yes.

"Why would you need to record this?" Tre asked a bit suspiciously.

"It's just for note taking, Bo said sensing his hesitation. Our attorney/ client privileges protects this conversation from going anywhere outside of these walls, he said looking around at the walls as he took a seat across from Tre at his desk. This recorder just frees me up is all, from having to write down everything. I get much more data to work with this way. He smiled at Tre one of those reassuring smiles that says trust me, everything will be just fine. Tre never returned his smile. Instead he hopped up from his seat and walked out of the room. He returned several seconds later producing his own recorder he used from time to time to record beats on the road. He took his seat back at the desk and sat his recorder right next to Bo's.

"Well if that's the case, I'm sure you don't mind me recording this session either?" Bo laughed at that gesture. He leaned back in his chair and crossed his leg high at the knee, he replied . . . "nope…not at all"

———

"Looks like I got all the information I need at this time" Bo said, looking down at his watch as he stood up. Both men shook hands across the desk. Tre felt a lot more at ease than when the meeting first began.

"Yeah I got another client coming in myself, he should be here any second" Tre said eyeing the time on his laptop computer sitting beside him on the desk.

"Who is it?" Bo asked…A look of excitement crossing his face. Tre laughed.

"It's nobody you'd know…not yet anyways. He's a rising star… in preparation."

"Oh"… Bo said a bit disappointed. He was hoping to catch another glimpse of someone famous, this way he'd have a double scoop of excitement to share with his daughter on the ride home. Bo walked to the door as Tre followed him.

"I'm not saying this case will be a slam dunk one, but I'm confident I can keep you and your friend Mike out of the slammer. It may cost you both a hefty fine, so be prepared for this. You'll both take a hit in the pocket before it's all said and done, but it shouldn't ruin you. Your reputation is the most important thing to keep here."

Bo liked to be as up front and honest with his clients as possible, he learned early on in his career that his high profile clients preferred it this way.

"I'll work to make sure the hit is as soft as possible. Depending upon who's judging is gonna determine the amount of the fine you pay. Some judges are more lenient than others….But you didn't hear me say that" Looking back to see if Tre's recorder was far enough away that it didn't catch what he'd just shared.

"Just be sure to have your assistant get me all your tax forms from the last seven years. I'll need them all. Tre shook his head in agreement. I'll also be needing your profit and loss sheets for the same time period. I'll have my paralegal send something to you via email stating all the forms we'll need. I'll be in touch. Bo reached for the door handle but there was someone forcing the door open from the opposite end. "tap tap tap" Carlos tapped on the door as he let himself in. Bo took a step back, allowing Carlos room to step in.

"Oh, my bad...I didn't see y'all right there" Carlos said as he came through the door, looking from Tre to Bo. Reds accompanied him, walking in behind Carlos, close on his heels. "Barbara said you were expecting me so she didn't call up."

"You must be the rising star!" Bo said to Carlos, extending his hand out for him to shake. Carlos seemed perplexed, but he went along with it, grinning he accepted Bo's hand shake. He was flattered Tre thought enough of him to have shared such a compliment with someone else.

"This here is my man Reds" he said, stepping out the way and allowing him to shake Reds hand as well. Tre stood there with his hands relaxed in his pockets, not interested in participating in the cordial gestures.

"What is it that you do?" Bo asked out of curiosity. Carlos gathered from the question that he must not have been the *topic* of their conversation, more like passing through it...

"Oh I aaaah...I do hip-hop songs, conscious music mainly."

"Ooh conscious rap!" Bo said, turning to look back over his shoulder at Tre, giving him a raised eyebrow and nod of approval.

"Well that's good news! We certainly need more *conscious* rappers out here representing today.... Well I won't hold you from your artistry... Good luck to you guys. I'll be looking forward to hearing the finished work."

"Thanks!" Carlos said. Once Bo left, Tre turned his attention over to them.

"Don't I know you from someplace?" He asked Reds.

"Yeah...Reds said nervously. "I was here for the album release party in the fall."

Tre thought on it for a moment. "Ooooh yeah, that's right, you were the one posted up in the corner all night with...with...*his* girl Crystal." Everyone who knew of Tre, knew he was not the one to hold back his thoughts. At that moment the tension in the room became so thick you could cut it with a knife. After a long moment of silence Tre spoke up.

"What!"..."what did I say?" Amused at himself, he looked back and forth from both men.

"What are we working on?" Carlos asked as he made his way towards the music board, ignoring the question in an attempt to lead the conversation away from the danger zone. "I got you geared up and ready for part two of the track" Tre said. "I've been working on some stuff over the weekend, some new sounds I want to try out on you.

Reds settled down onto the couch, not bothering to wait to be offered a seat.

"Let's do this!" said Carlos.

———◆———

Reds was thoroughly impressed with his friend. He'd heard Carlos freestyle on numerous occasions and knew without a doubt he was extremely talented, but this was his first time witnessing him work at a professional level. He felt like a groupie.

It was well after midnight, but the adrenalin was at such high levels that none of them noticed the time.

"I can't tell you enough how impressed I am with your skills." Tre told him as he began shutting down the electricity running to the sound board.

"Most new artists I work with need twice as much studio time to complete their first album. We're almost done. You're a natural at this." Carlos grinned, trying not to lead on how important that made him feel.

"Where's your manager?" Tre asked. "I haven't seen that dude since we signed? What is he doing?" Carlos gave Tre a side eyed look. They'd been working together long enough to have built a small level of friendliness amongst each other.

"Man I told you I hired him only because *you* insisted. What is he *supposed* to be doing? Besides staying out my way."

Tre chuckled, "Where did you find him anyways? Craigslist?" They all laughed.

"Seriously though man," Tre chimed, you *will* need a good manager, I can do but so much as a producer. You may be good for now, but life *will* become a lot more hectic for you once album sales begin to climb. You'll need someone reliable around to handle your day to day affairs. So if it's not gonna be that dude, then you'll need to find *somebody* reliable to manage you."

"You can't just refer someone to me?" Carlos asked.

Tre looked at him and chuckled. "You got a lot of faith in me youngin, some of that faith you should have in yourself. I'm confident you'll find a good fit when the need arises. By the way, have you spoken to my baby about your intro video?" Carlos shot Reds a horrified look, begging for salvation with his eyes.

"Not yet" He said under his breath.

"Not yet!"..."What the hell you waitin' on man? You need to be working on that like yesterday! Here, where's my phone? Tre began patting his body and looking around his work station for his cell phone.

"What you bout to do?" Carlos asked, growing irritated.

"Ima call her now while I have you here…"

"It's *after midnight* Tre man…Don't do that!" Carlos's voice went from irritation to outright anger. He saw Reds out the corner of his eye cover his face with both hands, not wanting to witness what was about to take place. Tre was startled by his anger…

"Who you basin at?" He asked him, returning the same energy Carlos had put out.

Carlos gave himself a few moments to cool down. "I'm just saying it's late, you aint gotta call her this time of night, I'll call her in the morning, I'll take care of it." Tre gave him a long hard stare. He was beginning to sense something wasn't quite right but he couldn't place his finger on the hot button.

"I need to speak with her anyways." He said more to himself than to Carlos. "She's been ducking me here lately and I don't know why."

Tre located his phone sitting off to the side of the keyboard where he left it earlier. He reached over and grabbed it and began dialing Tammy. Carlos turned to face Reds, he was fuming. Fist clinched he walked towards Reds who was still sitting wide eyed and stiffly on the couch. His back was turned so Tre couldn't see the words he mouthed to his friend..."Ima kill this mother fuc***!"

"Hey Tammy...what you doing girl" Tre spoke confidently into the phone. Carlos plopped down hard on the couch beside his friend. He leaned back and folded his arms tightly across his chest. Reds could feel the heat coming from his friends body.

"Hold up...ima put you on speaker" Tre sat the phone down on top of the keyboard and hit the speaker button on it. Tammy's voice went bellowing across the room...

"Why are you calling me this late Tre....What? What do you want? She said half-heartedly.

"Aye I'm here with your girl's peeps....Cee-los and aaaah aaaah"

"Reds"...Reds helped him.

"Yeah and... Reds" Tre said.

"What's up with his intro video?" The silence in the room grew deafening. No one spoke a word. After a very long uncomfortable silence Tre finally spoke up.

"Hello...Hello you still there? He picked up the phone to check its reception.

"Yeah I'm here" Tammy said sullenly.

"Did you hear me? What's up with Cee's video? He asked her again. Tre why are you calling me with this? It's late!" She said irritated.

"Well damn, what's up with all the funky attitudes today?"....Tre said throwing his hands up in the air, looking over at Carlos who was sitting there looking like a pint up panther locked in an imaginary cage.

"I can't get you on the phone no other time, so I figured I'd try you now. Why you aint been answering my calls anyhow, I've been calling you for the past two weeks, you gone make me pop up on you girl." Reds closed his eyes again, placing his hands over them. He could feel Carlos's leg beside him moving restlessly, it began shaking the whole couch.

"I'm not doing this with you" Tammy said right before she hung.

"Hello!!! Hello!!!" Tre said as he looked down at the phone in his hand shocked and embarrassed. She had never hung up on him before. He was not prepared for it.

"Let's go." Carlos said to Reds as they both stood up to leave. Reds couldn't get to the door fast enough. Tre looked over at them and back to the phone in total shock and confusion.

"I'm out!" Was all Carlos said before walking out the door. Tre sat there long after they left, replaying the scene back over and over in his mind.

CHAPTER 14

———◆———

TAMMY WAS UP PACING THE floor. She placed her bottom lip in between her teeth with the same hand that held the phone. She bit down gently as she walked back and forth barefoot across the floor of her tiny bedroom. She wasn't sure what to do. She and Carlos had just gotten back on good terms and now this... She was concerned about his feelings. Did Tre know? Were they talking about her now? Is the whole bag of beans spilled? She was a basket case. She wanted to call Carlos but wasn't sure if he was still there with Tre. Not knowing what else to do she reached down and dialed Crystal's number. Crystal answered groggily on the fourth ring.

"He-llo"

"Crystal...hey Crystal please wake up...I need someone to talk to."

"You better be dying someplace on the side of the road" Crystal said in between sleep.

"No, I'm home...but I need to talk, you up?"

"No I'm not *up*. This better be good Tam." Tammy ignored her last remark. "Girl why Tre just called me on speaker phone with Carlos in the room!" Crystal could never resist a good soap opera, she sat up in her bed.

"He did what!" She stammered through the phone. "when?"

"Yes! Just now! I aint know what to do, so I hung up on him."

"You did *what?*" Crystal said...wide awoke at this point.

156

"I knoooooooow" Tammy said, her voice full of guilt. I aint know what else to do!"

"Lawd have mercy girl….Where is Carlos? Have you talked to him?"

"No. I didn't want to call him because I wasn't sure if he was still there with Tre."

Crystal began thinking fast for a solution. She couldn't help it. Being a successful business owner, she was always in solution mode.

"So what did Tre call you for?" She asked, gathering more information for her investigative report.

"Something about Carlos's video, but Carlos and I already spoke about that, so I'm not sure why he would've called me so late about it? I think it was a cover up to get me on the phone. But I didn't hang around to find out. I got nervous and hung up."

"Girl I swear…you and these men" Crystal said shaking her head.

"You and I both know Tre is not the type to go beating around the bush, I doubt if it was a set up. I don't know *how* you think you gonna keep this madness going Tammy. And when Tre *does* finally put all the pieces together, how you think he's gonna react? You should really think about that!"

"Don't you think I *have* Cryss…It's either his feelings or Carlos's career, and right now Carlos takes precedence.

"What about *your* career?" Crystal said firmly. "This man has the ability to *destroy* your career with one press conference! Have you taken *that* into consideration?"

Tammy sighed in defeat.

"I can only hope that he wouldn't do that."

'Hope! Hope???...You're hanging onto a hope and a prayer? You are really playing with fire girlfriend. I say tell him, and the sooner the better."

"I *am* gonna tell him!" Tammy found herself growing frustrated. She was beginning to regret she even called Crystal. "But not right now. When Carlos gets this record finished and its been promoted…*then* I'll tell him."

"So you're using the man?" Crystal asked.

"No I'm not using him, he's benefitting too! He wouldn't even be working with Carlos if he wasn't sure he'd benefit in the long run. Tre is a business man, above all else. I'm not using him. Besides, I don't *owe* him anything!"

"If you don't owe him anything then you'd tell him...now!" Just then Tammy's line buzzed, it was Carlos calling.

"Oh shit girl this is Carlos calling me now...Ima call you back"

"No you aint!" Crystal said. Call me in the morning, I aint losing no more sleep over this mess. Call Tre when you get off with him, that's my advice...bye!"

"Hello!" Tammy answered sheepishly. Not knowing what his mood would be.

"Why you hang up on that dude?" Carlos said in a light hearted tone. Tammy was relieved that he didn't sound upset.

"I didn't know what else to do" she said honestly.

"Where are you?" she asked him.

"In the car with Reds, on my way home."

"Won't you ask Reds to drop you off over here instead?" Carlos thought about it for a second before he responded;

"Naaaw, I'm tired...I'm going home." Tammy was crushed. She hadn't remembered Carlos ever rejecting her advances. She wasn't sure what to make of it. Not wanting to add to any stresses of the day she let it go.

"Okay she said. You wanna just call me back when you get in?"

"No ima hit the sack hard tonight, I just wanted to know why you hung up on him the way you did? That was kind of suspect."

"Suspect?" she repeated. "What do you mean?"

"I mean why would you hang up if you don't have anything to hide?"

Tammy realized then what he was alluding to, her fears heightening.

"Carlos what are you suggesting?" She asked him sternly.

"I aint suggesting nothing, I just asked you a simple question!"

"Really? *Really?*... You are questioning me about that man?" Carlos didn't reply. Instead he waited for her to elaborate. When she didn't his suspicions grew further.

"Well?"

"Well what!" She answered.

"Why did you hang up so *quick*?" Tammy felt trapped in a corner. It was damned if she did, damned if she didn't. Every move she made when it came to Tre backfired in her face. She felt helpless to fix all the broken pieces that were beginning to scatter about her feet. She felt emotionally drained.

"Listen Carlos" she said, I'm not gonna fight with you tonight over nothing.

"Who's fighting?" He said, matching her annoyance. She continued...

"Its late...very late. I was hoping to see you tonight, but now I see that your *distrust* for me is preventing that from happening. Can we just agree to sleep off these frustrations and discuss it further in the morning?"

"So you gonna hang up on *me too* huh?" He said sarcastically. Tammy breathed a heavy sigh.

"*Nooo Carlos*, I have no intentions on hanging up on you. I just don't wanna fight, especially over nothing."

"Over *nothing* huh?" He said. "I have to sit in that man's face and listen to him dote over you and watch his eyes light up when he says your name, and I'm just supposed to sit there and deal with it huh? But it's *nothing* to you huh?"

"Don't twist my words Carlos! That's not fair!"

"*Fair!*....Did I hear you just say what's not *fair*?" Tammy wanted to cry. She had no place to escape, trapped in her own web of deceit.

"What do you want me to say?" She asked him in a defeated tone.

"I don't want you to say anything, you've said enough. He said harshly. It's what you should be *doing!*" Tammy felt like the world was against her. She understood Tre far better than he did, and she knew that he would never be accepting of their relationship. She knew first-hand how he would react, so she was hell bent on protecting him.

"Carlos it's late…please can we discuss this tomorrow?" She begged, she simply wanted the pressure to cease.

"If you don't tell him Tam, then I will!"

"Tell him *what?*" She said raising her voice. I thought you and I agreed we were taking things slow anyways?" Now it was Carlos's turn to be crushed. He sat quietly on the line, taking in what she had just said. Tammy knew she was playing with fire, taking a huge risk with her words, but she felt she had no other choice. Telling Tre the truth this late in the game was *not* an option she was willing to take. She just hoped she could keep her relationship with Carlos intact throughout the process.

"Okay Tammy," he said depressingly. "I'll talk to you later."

"Are you upset with me?" She asked. Carlos breathed a heavy sigh before responding…"No I'm not upset with you. Disappointed… but not upset." Tammy was relieved. She could live with the disappointment, for now.

"I'm sorry to disappoint you Carlos, truly I am. Please let me handle this thing with Tre. I promise you it'll all work itself out in the end, but you have to trust me on this one. Let me handle him, *pleeeease.*" She pleaded, trying one last time to get her point across. Carlos didn't bother to respond to her plead.

"Good night Tammy." He said in a defeated tone…"I'll talk to you tomorrow."

Tammy decided not to push it any further, she said good night as they both hung up.

Carlos looked over at Reds as he drove. Reds shook his head in disgust.

"Man this thing is getting outta hand Los, they got this dude thinking that you and *Crystal* got a thing. There's so many lies floating around I can't keep up wit em any more!"

"I know man," Carlos said as he thought hard on it. "Its fucked up."

"That dude aint stupid man" Reds added.

"Did you see how he looked at you before we left?" He looked from the road over at Carlos, driving his point home. "I bet he's putting all this shit together in his head right now as we speak."

"And once he finds out, he's gonna think you all were *pimpin* him! Man, this aint a good look...at all Los!"

"Yeah I know" Carlos said under his breath. He thought hard on Reds' words.

"I'm mad at myself for allowing it to go this far. I feel like a *sucker*. But I guess at this point, its gonna boil down to how bad I want this album released."

CHAPTER 15

———————

NANA SAT WATCHING THE WOMAN across from her. They were at Per Se, a French restaurant overlooking the Hudson River. She sat there regally, perfect shoulders back, head held high peering over at the mystery woman through her reading glasses. Both women ordered a simple glass of wine, skipping the main course out of uncertainty on how the meeting would go. Nana watched her carefully. Her beautiful dark complexion glinting perfectly off the white of her linen suit jacket. Her short tightly kinked hair picked up a hint of brown from the sun rays seeping through the window where they sat. Nana couldn't help but to notice how smooth her skin was, she appeared not to have aged a second.

Nana watched her as she fiddled nervously with the crisp linen napkin in front of her. She wore a simple gold band on her wedding finger, around her neck was a thin gold chain that held a small gold locket. One of those lockets that captured photographs, glimpses of memories in time. The locket was closed shut. From the naked eye it appeared to be just a simple piece of jewelry, but Nana had a suspicion that it held more secrets than a Pandora's Box. She sat quietly, stealthily, watching her every move … Nana did not shield her suspicions, deliberately piercing the younger woman's skin with her eyes. It was not a meeting of pleasantries and Nana had no intentions of pretending that it was. Having nothing to say, she waited, like a patient lioness for the dark mystery woman to speak.

Finally she looked… into Nana's eyes, the eyes she had been eluding the whole while they were there. Thirty years of pain came gushing through a single glance. The woman in the white linen suit picked the napkin up off the table in front of her, she placed her face inside of it and wept. She wept quietly yet profusely, exposing her deep rooted pain. She wept and wept for what seemed like forever. Nana never moved. She didn't speak a word. She sat across from her in stiff silence, the patience of a God…watching her intently as she wept.

The waitress came over to replenish their wine glasses. She noticed the woman crying and upon instinct went to place her hand onto her shoulder in comfort, Nana lifted her hand from its relaxed position on her lap and held her palm facing out towards the waitress, as if to say… back off! She had spoken volumes with one swift motion. The waitress took one look into Nana's regal eyes and did as she was commanded, she turned and walked away from the table. Finally the woman stopped her crying. She wiped the remaining tears onto the napkin before blowing her nose in it. She pulled her slumped back up from the table, taking in a deep breath. Her eyes were red and puffy, her nose swollen. She looked over at Nana, speaking for the first time.

"Thank you for agreeing to see me." Her accent was heavy in her native tongue….She continued….

"How is she?"

"She is doing just fine" Nana responded matter of factly.

"May I please see a picture? Do you have a photo please?" The woman pleaded.

Nana thought for a second, deciding to grant her wish, she reached over and pulled her wallet from her purse sitting on the empty chair beside her. She pulled a small wallet size photograph from it, placed it on the table in front of her and pushed it gently over towards the puffy eyed woman. She picked it up as if it was fine crystal, studying the face that smiled back at her from a perfect point position. The woman gasped in excitement,

"She's a dancer!...a dancer...just like you!" Nana nodded in proud agreements.

"Does she have children?" the woman asked desperately. Nana sensed where the conversation was headed, and decided to take the reins instead.

"Why did you come back here...After all this time?" The woman glanced up quickly at Nana, sensing the sudden shift in mood. She breathed a heavy sigh, lowering her head in shame.

"I never stopped loving her. I never stopped missing her." she said.

"I think of her...all the time, every day. That is why I am back here... she said taking the picture and coddling it on her lap.

Nana couldn't help but to feel somewhat connected to her pain, somewhere inside of her own belly, she panged for this woman....

"What is your interest here now...with *us.*" Nana asked her, putting emphasis on the last word, allowing her to know that Tammy was never alone, that she had plenty of love, plenty to help offset those feelings of abandonment she *must've* felt at times.

"I'd just like to see her, if I may. I need her to know that I love her, that I never stopped loving her...I.... I could not live with myself another day." The woman said...choking back more tears.

"You *do* know that you can ruin a child by doing what you did?" *"Do* you know this?" Nana asked her harshly, leaving no guesses as to where her loyalty lied.

"I do know...I do understand the role I played, I'm not proud of myself, the lady said snapping back at Nana for the first time all night. The lady knew she was to come through Nana first, before even seeing her son, before anyone else. She knew from her upbringing in her village that she was to go to the matriarch of the family first, out of respect for the elders. Here she was, thousands of miles from home, in a land that was as strange and foreign to her as the first time she was on these shores.

"I understand what you have gone through, what I have put you and Sam, you all through." Sounding sincerely remorseful.

"I'm here because my heart is broken and I need to see my daughter...please understand." She looked up at Nana in search of sympathy. Nana sighed. Shaking her head in displeasure. She knew she couldn't realistically keep this woman away from her own daughter, nor would she even try. She just wanted her to be fully aware of the dangers this Pandora's box could open.

"What are your intentions once you satisfy your craving? Nana asked her defensively. "Is your plan to walk out on her again?" That stung her right in the chest, but she remained steady.

"No! I never plan to leave her again...if she'll have me." Those last words barely spoken, but there none the less, hanging in the air like thick fog.

"I want to remain in touch with her...from now on."

"How are we to know this is true? That your intentions are genuine? That child has been hurt enough...I will NOT allow you to waltz back into her life only to cause more damage!" The pretty dark skinned woman reached in her purse and pulled out a small thin leather booklet. She reached over to hand it to Nana. Not sure of what it was, Nana didn't move. So she placed it on the plate in front of the old woman. Nana looked down and saw that its cover read "passport."

"I am prepared to stay here as long as it takes to see my daughter!" The woman said, quiet tears streaming down her face. Nana had heard enough. Her concern was strictly for the emotional well-being of Tammy, she wanted to protect her, at all cost. It was clear that this woman's pain was thick with remorse. Nana knew deep down that this day would one day come, she knew these were the jolts that life promised you, those whirlwinds that you could not take cover from, the ones you had to simply ride out.

Nana sighed. "I will speak with her father about this tonight. Are you staying here?" Nana asked, looking around the room with her eyes.

"Yes" the lady responded quickly.

"Share with me your room number and I will call you this evening." She was relieved. Wiping her tears swiftly she reached back into her purse and pulled out an ink pen. She wrote the number down on a napkin, the first thing she saw in front of her. She wrote in a hurry, as if Nana may change her mind about the whole idea at any second. She picked the napkin up, carefully laying it in Nana's waiting palm.

"Thank You" is all she said as she watched her stand slowly, using the arms of the Victorian chair to pull her senior years up with her. She left the passport where it lay, there on the table.

"Oh here's your photo back" The lady reached down and grabbed it from her lap, extending it out to her. Nana ignored her request. She grabbed her gold tip cane from the back of the chair, "use it to update that there locket around your neck" she said, before turning and slowly walking away...

CHAPTER 16

CRYSTAL FLUNG THE COMB AT Amina's head playfully. "I swear girl ima fire you one of these days. If you don't go do what I asked... you better!" One of Crystal's regular clients sat in her chair, laughing at them both.

"You see this Ms. Nancy? Amina pointing an accusing finger at Crystal as she quickly backed away.

"I'm telling ya'al she's violent! I'm scared for my life up in here most days." Both women laughed at that. Amina was a clown. It was one of the things that drew Crystal to her from the beginning. Crystal hired her on the spot during their interview process partly due to her bubbly personality. She had two more girls to interview for the position after Amina but Crystal knew immediately she would be the one. She never even bothered interviewing the others. It had been two years sense then and Crystal hadn't doubted her decision once. The gap in their ages allowed Crystal to be a role model to her. The relationship between them resembled more of a sisterhood than anything else. Crystal loved Amina, and wanted nothing but the best for her. She worked steadily to foster her potential. If only she could keep her from being so silly... *all* the time.

"How many times do I have to tell you to get your assignments completed *before* you come over here asking for favors? You won't be able to get away with that crap with anyone else...Nobody's gonna wanna hire you always looking for a favor. Get your work done first! "

"That's why I aint gonna work for nobody else" Amina shot back. Ima work with you and learn from you and open my own shop one day…right next door…and be your competition!"

Both ladies laughed again.

"You see what I gotta put up with around here?" Crystal said to her client, shaking her head as she began twisting her hair again. Inwardly she was amused to hear Amina talk like that. She wanted nothing more than to see her favorite assistant soar like an eagle. It made her feel good to know she'd be helping her to fly. She knew Amina could do it too…run her own shop. She had the spunk and the drive. Amina was self-confident and could be very professional when she wasn't kidding around. She had a good command of the language, and was great at settling disputes and maintaining high levels of customer satisfaction. All the things Crystal knew she would need in order to run a success-ful business on her own. Crystal figured in another two to three years, Amina would be ready to manage her own shop. She'd even toyed with the idea of expanding the business and allowing Amina to join in as a partner. Crystal never shared these thoughts with her though, she kept them to herself. She knew that if she'd ever said anything to her about it, Amina would bug her half to death until those two to three years turned into two to three months!….Oh she was ambitious alright.

"And get your aunt Tammy on the line for me please." She said aloud before Amina could get out of earshot. A few moments later Amina leaned her head from behind the glass partition that separated the front desk area from the rest of the shop.

"I called her…she said she was out and she'd call you a little later."

Crystal looked over at the clock on the rose colored wall, it read seven o'seven.

"Hmgh"…Crystal said to no one in particular. She knew her best friend well, she wouldn't be at the studio this time of evening on a Wednesday. She figured there was no other place Tammy could be than with Carlos. A slight pang of jealousy crossed her chest. Crystal thought maybe she and Tammy could go out for a glass of wine tonight. Being as though she was just about finished with her last client. It was something they did together regularly, but Tammy hadn't had much time to spend with her lately. Crystal liked Carlos, he was a good match for her friend. But she couldn't help but to feel as if she were competing for Tammy's attention these days. Crystal didn't particularly like how this felt. These new feelings were met with some resentment.

"Okay thanks!" Crystal shouted across the room, letting Amina know she'd heard her.

———◆———

Tammy sat across from her father at the kitchen table, the very same spot where she'd read the first postcard. The only difference was her Grandmother had joined them for a seat at the table this time. Two postcards sat in front of her, one atop the other. A napkin with hand written digits scribbled across it lay neatly beside the postcards. Tammy breathed heavily for the umpteenth time that evening...

"I still don't understand why you guys are trying to make me do this" she said, her tone filled with irritation. It was her father who replied.

"Tammy, nobody here is *making* you do anything. Your grandmother and I felt it would be in your best interest to at least *meet* with her. We thought you might have questions that you've always wanted answers to?" Tammy shot him a frown.

"*Questions!*" All the MILLION and one questions I had for her I dismissed from my mind a long, loooong time ago. I don't care about her answering any questions for me, and I'm not interested in meeting with her!" It was her grandmother's turn to speak.

"That's not a good attitude to take kitten" she said in a calm soothing tone.

"What you're displaying now is escapism. You may *think* you've gotten over her absence all these years, but you have not. I think this meeting, with her, your mother, would be healthy for you. It'll help you heal some deep seated wounds."

"HEAL? What WOUNDS???" Tammy said raising her tone a little louder than before. I can *assure* you I don't have any wounds Nana...I'm fiiiiine goshhhhhhh! She said growing even more frustrated.

"If you're so fine, why all the reservations about meeting her? Why won't you just go....if there's no problem?" Tammy tried to think of a good answer but had none. She contemplated what her Nana said, really considering it for the first time that night. She was so busy defending her stance that she hadn't even considered "why" she had such a stance. They sat there, unmoved, watching her intently, neither of them speaking. It was almost as if they knew she needed this moment to think through her feelings. Finally after almost a full minute had passed, Tammy breathed in heavily. She looked over at her grandmother and then to her father, scanning both their faces in search of hidden answers that neither could give her.

"Alright"...she said...defeated. "Alright...I'll go."

"But you have to go with me Nana cause you're the only one who knows what this...this... lady looks like, I don't!" Nana knew this was her way of asking for moral support. Her pride would never allow her to come out and say it, but Nana understood.

"Yes...I'll go with you"...She replied.

The next morning Tammy exited the cab in front of the hotel. She reached back to help Nana out with her cane.

"And this is the one?" Tammy asked, looking back across her shoulder at the sprawling thirty story building towering above her head.

"Yes, this is the one" she said, as she scooted herself slowly out of the cab. We used to dance in that theatre right down the road there when I was your age, pointing as she stood. "All the white performers who came in from out of town used to stay in this here hotel. She thanked the cab driver, shutting the door behind her.

"I would go over with them sometimes for a cocktail after the show. I remember how those bartenders used to stare at me so angrily." Nana chuckled, "I guess they thought they could growl me up outta there. I'd just smile at em nicely, and ask for another drink." Nana chucked again, as she thought back. "Those were treacherous times," she added.

"Where's she gonna be?" Tammy asked as they started towards the front entrance. Nana recognized the caution in Tammy's voice. "She'll be meeting us in the lobby, kitten. If memory serves me, there's a large seating area on the back patio of the hotel. Once we see her, we'll head there.

Nana called Tammy's mother the night before to inform her that they'd both be coming. Nana decided on meeting at another hotel altogether, so they'd be on equal grounds, a place unfamiliar to both of them. She understood *location* was sometimes as important as the meeting itself. The time was eight forty-five as they walked into the lobby, they were fifteen minutes early. Tammy looked pretty as usual. She wore a soft yellow sundress that landed at her knees to match the late August weather. It was one of Tammy's favorite dresses. She put it on just so her mother could see she hadn't missed a beat. She wanted her to understand clearly, even in her dress, that things were just fine without her.

Tammy scanned the crowd looking for any black face she could find. Nana felt tension on her arm where Tammy was subconsciously applying pressure.

"Breathe darling...just breathe...." Nana said, patting her elbow softly as they made their way to the lobby seating area. Not realizing she'd stopped breathing, Tammy took her grandmothers advice and in hailed deeply.

"We're a bit early, I don't see her so let's wait over here" Nana said, pointing to a bright colored loveseat over near a sprawling fountain in the middle of the lobby. Tammy was an emotional wreck. She surprised even herself at her reaction, she didn't anticipate being this jittery.

"Nana why am I nervous?" she said half-jokingly.

"It's a normal reaction kitten," she said reassuring her. "I'd be nervous too if I were in your shoes. You're gonna be fine, it'll all work itself out in the end." They both took a seat and waited in silence.

It was nine o'clock on the nose when the automatic doors of the front lobby sprung open and a woman in a flawless African printed suit stepped in. She stopped right after the threshold, taking off her tiger print sunshades, she scanned the lobby with her eyes. She appeared much younger than her actual 53 years. She could've easily been mistaken for a spunky young urbanite, here to do a cover shoot for a fashion magazine than an aging mother of *two* adult children. She had style, a trait Tammy seemingly picked up naturally.

She spotted them and quickly made her way over to where they were seated. Tammy caught a glimpse of her midway and their eyes locked. Her fears went from a four to a ten in one flat second as her heart began pounding out of her chest. The woman, her mother began to weep. She reached her daughter and gently laid her clutch that perfectly matched her sunshades on the couch beside Tammy. Never once taking her eyes off her. She wanted to grab Tammy and squeeze her but she was afraid of what the reaction might be, so she asked through her tears,

"Can I hug you? Please? Tammy?" Tammy hesitated briefly before shaking her head in agreements. She reached for her daughter desperately as the two women embraced. They held each other, chest to chest, arms embraced for what seemed like forever. Tammy's heart pounded through her chest as tears streamed down her mother's face. There was no doubt this woman never stopped loving her child.

Finally Nana spoke, "Let's make our way to the back patio" she said, compassion filling her voice. She grabbed her daughter's hand gently and used the other to wipe away her tears. They followed Nana out past the hotel lobby, into the sun room towards the rear. Nana was an astute elder. She'd resolved all her differences with her the day before. She held no malice in her heart, she was wise enough to understand that would be useless energy. She had no intentions on making this moment any more difficult for Tammy than necessary. Her goal in mind was to help bring peace to the situation. They found an empty table out near the garden. It was a beautiful scene, the lilies and dandelions were in full bloom as their pedals touched the hems of the crabapple trees. The rod iron patio sets matched the flowers perfectly. Nana excused herself as the other two took their seats. She made up something about having to find the lady's room, wanting to give them both some space alone to feel out the moment.

"You look amazing" her mother said in her strong native tongue. Oh my goodness, I am just so grateful to you for seeing me. I have so much to say to you, my tongue is tied, she chuckled nervously. Tammy waited to hear more...

"I know you're probably upset with me, for a lot of reasons." Tammy shrugged her shoulders unconvincingly.

"I realize I've lost out on a lot of time, that I can't get back, but I need you to know that I always carried you right here." She placed her hand over her chest. Tammy noticed the small gold band on her wedding finger.

"I thought of you every single day."

"It's been twenty nine years sense you *left* us," Tammy surprised herself at the sharpness of her tone. "What made you decide to look for me now?" Her mother sighed heavily, sitting back in her chair, she contemplated what she'd say. She never kidded herself into thinking this reunion was gonna be anything but difficult. She had a lot of time...years, DECADES to prepare for this moment. A few more seconds passed, before she spoke.

"You know I rehearsed this moment a thousand times in my head. I guess you can never be fully prepared for a moment like this. Did your father ever share with you any stories of my life? I mean in Africa before I come here to America?" Tammy shook her head no. Not trusting her words enough to speak them aloud.

"Please, allow me then... I was born in Soweto. Back when it was tough...real tough to be a young girl seeking a decent education. It was this way for most young girls in many parts of South Africa. To make a long *looong* story short, when I was younger, in school, the government where I lived began forcing us students to learn all of our curriculums in the English language, a language none of us Soweto girls were accustomed to." Tammy didn't understand where this story was leading to, and what it had to do with her, but she listened intently anyways.

"We didn't want that. We wanted to learn our lessons in our own language. The language of our parents tongue, and *their* parents tongue. We would argue with the white settlers who came to teach us this new curriculum but no one would listen. Our pleas went unheard until one day me and a couple of other classmates decided to organize a protest around it. We never dreamed at the time that our actions would cause such a stir. We got some other students involved and boycotted the school one day. We left the school courtyard and began marching and chanting in unison through the streets. The next thing you know, more students from another nearby school, and other young people whose parents were unable to afford school tuition and were left in the fields to crop for the season heard our chants and decided to join in. After some time, there were "many, several hundred" young people marching alongside us! Many gathered, before long we had a great crowd. Finally, after several hours of marching we reached a road where the police had set up a blockade. There were many…many policeman all around it."

Tammy hung on tightly to her every word.

"They blocked the road where we could not pass. And when they did this, those who walked with us in solidarity became unruly. We tried to settle them down but our voices were washed out in the crowd, there were just too many of us present. Some of the boys began throwing rocks at the policeman, soon after that shots rang out."

She paused and looked up at Tammy. Her expression changing. She was remembering a painful part of her past. She went on…

"We all ran, we began running and screaming to take cover, as the policeman continued shooting out into the crowd." Tammy gasped, bringing her mother back into the present.

She looked at Tammy with weary in her eyes.

"When it was all over, there were dead bodies everywhere." Tammy covered her mouth with her hand in shock.

"After that day, my parents got word that government officials were looking for those who helped to organize the march. I was one of them. My parents were not sure what would happen to me, why they wanted to find me so they thought it best if I got as far away from my home as possible. This is how I ended up here, in America. I was smuggled out of my country and came to live with friends of my family while I was here, until I met your father. After I left, the villagers concocted up a story and told the officials I was amongst the dead, and that they buried me right away as was customary in my culture.

"Does dad know all this?" Tammy asked in a hushed whisper.

"No! He does not know all of the details. I could not tell anyone why I was really in America. This government here was helping the apartheid regime in my country. They were in cahoots. I could not risk being caught so I told no one my story. I held it inside of me. When I met your father, he was so kind to me. The kindest man I ever met. He helped to take my mind off my past. He was very good to me. Better than anyone had been to me in this Country. It was easy for me to fall in love with him. It was a scary time in my life. I leaned on him a lot for emotional support and he was very compassionate. I lived with the thought every day that someone would find out who I was and turn me in."

She leaned back in the chair, reflecting on all she'd endured.

"Why did you leave? To go back home?" Tammy wanted to know more. Her mother's somber voice returned to the story.

"My parent's friends here in America received a call one day that my father was very ill. I was told that they did not think he would make it through his illness. I did not know what to do. By this time you were already birthed and the three of us were building a life together. But I still missed home very much. When I received the news about my father's ailing health, I couldn't live with myself not being there with him.

175

I blamed myself for his being sick. I convinced myself that it was me who had caused him great stress, causing him to become deathly ill."

"But you didn't do anything wrong." Tammy said confusingly. She looked up at Tammy and grinned.

"Right and wrong gets tossed all in a pot together in those type of moments. It became troublesome for me to live with myself. I fell into a deep *deep* depression. Deeper than before. I wanted to be home, and I wanted to be with you and your father too. After a while the depression became so severe that I wasn't well enough to care for you and your father properly. On top of this I was not able to express my true feelings to anyone. It was a tough time for me here. There were many days when I was too weak to even make it out of bed. Your grandmother stepped in and helped out when she could. I could not get my father out of my head. Eventually, I decided I must go back home to be with him." She looked over at Tammy, the pain of it all resonating on her face.

"I wanted to take you, I swear in my heart I wanted you with me." She began to cry.

"I was afraid for your own safety. And I couldn't tell your father. I was so torn." She began crying heavily. At that moment Tammy felt something for her besides resentment. She couldn't help but to feel her pain, her mother's pain. Tears of her own welled up in the corner of her eyes. Just then Nana returned, leaning heavily on her cane with each slow step. They both noticed her presence and used that moment to straighten up.

"Do you need me to give you both more space? Nana asked looking from one to the other.

"No...No, its okay" Tammy's mother said quickly, as she patted her eyes with the balled up tissue she retrieved from her purse.

"Please have a seat" she said extending her hand out towards the empty chair on the opposite end of the table. She sighed heavily as Nana pulled up the seat. Tammy remained silent, still taking in all she had just heard.

"Ms. Carolynn, I don't think I had the opportunity yesterday to say how grateful I am to you, and Sam for being there and filling the space of my absence. I understand there is nothing I could do to repay you, but I am grateful." Nana nodded her head in acceptance. Looking at her face she knew there was no need to add to the turmoil of her troubled soul. She spoke her name aloud for the first time.

"I only conducted myself as any grandmother would, Afua...as any grandmother would." Afua sighed as if a heavy weight was lifting from her shoulders. Sitting much taller in her chair she added,

"I will finish my story some other time if you don't mind. For now I would love this time to get to know *you* better. Please...tell me about yourself Tammy"....

CHAPTER 17

———————

TRE AND MIKE SAT SIDE-BY-SIDE in stiff leather chairs across from the attorney in his downtown office. Bo spoke is swift terms, flipping through the deposition papers his legal assistant typed up that morning. Well guys, looks to me like you'll be walking away from this thing but it's gonna cost you some. He leaned back casually, placing one arm across the back of his chair. Appearing as if he carried on this type of conversation all the time, just another day at the office for him.

The lead attorney on the state's side gave me the thumbs up on a deal that will keep us out of the courts completely. This way you won't have to worry about fickle jurors or...clearing his throat... racist judges. But it's gonna mean a chip off the old block. Both men looked at each other, understanding full well what each word meant. It was Mike who spoke first.

"What are we talking?" he asked.

"Fifty K each," he responded casually. He looked from one man to the other, reading their faces for a response. Neither men spoke. Mike shifted his weight uncomfortably in his chair as Tre sat back hard against his.

"So let me get this straight" Mike spoke up again. If he and I come up with fifty grand each, we can walk away from this thing, no questions asked?"

"That's it!" Bo shot back quickly.

"How does that work?" Tre asked confusingly. Bo chuckled, shaking his head down at the papers, becoming frustrated at having to deal with amateurs.

"Don't worry yourself about all that" he said.

"Just know I certainly wouldn't be risking my own reputation if it weren't a solid deal." Tre understood what he was hearing, but he couldn't fathom this type of stuff actually went on outside of the mobster movies.

"When do you need the money?" Mike asked him. Tre sensed his friend had already made up his mind, he was playing ball, but Tre wasn't as easily convinced. He wanted to know more about what was going on, he wanted to see if he could at least counter the offer. He wasn't sure about it being so cut and dry. He felt trapped. He found himself growing angry again at the thought of allowing Mike to lead him down this winding road.

"Hole....hole....hold up here for a minute" Tre said holding his hands out in front of him as if he was pushing an invisible boulder back. Bo looked at him a little annoyed.

"My pockets are not that deep!" My money is tied up in these artists. I can't get to that type of cash like that." Tre was calling his bluff. He understood in business, you had to at times play a little poker. Bo's jaw grew stiff. He looked straight into Tre's eyes, sounding more shrewd than ever before....

"That's the set gage, and the needle is not moving!"

The friendly guy Tre met with a few weeks ago at his office was all but gone. A disappearing act! Replaced with a shark. Tre felt like he was starring in a game of two card monte.

"How much time?" Mike barged in, sounding frustrated with it all. Bo looked from Mike to Tre and then back down at the papers. He flipped through a few pages before adding, if your friend here needs more time, I could always push the case back a week or two.

"Two weeks would be good," Mike shot back swiftly. "We'll see you then." He pushed his chair back, tapping Tre on the leg as he stood, motioning for him to join his action. Bo reached out his hand for a shake. Tre knew at that moment, he was making a deal with the devil.

———

CHAPTER 18

———◆———

CARLOS SAT ON THE SQUEAKY bed in his dusty room contemplating his life choices. Feeling a mixture of sadness and unrest he tried forcing himself to focus on the brighter side. Tammy, his album, his man Reds in his corner . . . But as he looked around the room, and down at his worn out tennis shoes, in that moment his feelings weren't as confident as his thoughts. The house was unusually quiet. Normally there'd be noise blasting from some place. A TV on in another room, the stereo shouting tunes from the first floor window, the landlord's girlfriend cursing at the top of her lungs . . . something! But this night the house was eerily quiet. He was grateful for the silence, to be able to hear his mind. He reached over and grabbed the *Source* magazine laying on the nightstand beside his bed, a photo of a younger Tupac Shakur on the cover. The caption read, "The life of a GOAT" He'd purchased it because of his strong connection to the rapper. He thought of himself when he thought about the man that Tupac was. Troubled. Gifted. Passionate. Determined. He studied the photo, thinking back to the day he was murdered, what that felt like. His eyes began to well up with tears. He squeezed em tightly shut, forcing the tears back.

"Damn man...*a fuckin waste!*" he said, tossing the magazine onto the bed beside him. He sighed heavily, placing his hands up to massage his face. He thought about how much money he had left in the bank. He counted about thirty more days before he'd be sitting on empty, forty five possibly if he accounted for the bucket of change he had growing in his closet. He'd already borrowed money from Reds and didn't want to go back to him again. He knew he could reach out to Tammy for a loan but he wouldn't dare. His pride wouldn't allow him to take money from her. Besides this, he didn't want to scare her off by giving her any indication of just how tight things had become.

"Thirty whole days" He said aloud, startling himself from the crackle in his voice.

It was times like these that bought a good man to drastic measures. He remembered the drug dealer who lived around the corner. He saw him serving a few times as he passed him walking home from the train. He thought about going to holler at him. His probation officer's face quickly popped into his mind. He felt caught between a rock and a hard place.

He needed encouragement. He needed someone, anyone to tell him that things would be alright. He needed a strong hug, a shoulder rub, a soft kiss. The thought of this made his manhood rise. He looked over at the clock on the rickety nightstand. Seeing it was way too late to call Tammy he pulled at the drawstring on his waist pants. His bone hard manhood sprung up from his sweats like a jack in the box… He began stroking himself.…

CHAPTER 19

CRYSTAL SAT CROSS LEGGED ON the hardwood floor, her back up against the mirrored wall. She hung onto every word that came from Tammy's mouth. She kept repeating herself "wow" over and over again as Tammy gave her all the details of the meeting with her mother.

"So you're telling me you have a younger *brother!*" Crystal said, extending her neck out to accentuate her surprise.

"Yep!" Tammy said as she took off across the room doing circular arabesques. Tammy didn't have a class to tend to that day, but she woke that morning still tense with all she'd taken in the day before. She knew dancing would help to relieve her nerves, it was part of her soul, she needed it like a songstress needed vocal cords. Dance was her outlet, her entertainment, her passion *and* her income.

"Wow"....Crystal repeated again.

"So wait...so....is she coming back? How...when you gonna get to meet him?" Crystal stuttered.

"She said she was coming back in December," Tammy said...still dancing. The tone of her voice matching her motions.

"She gave me some pictures, wanna see em?" She stopping her flailing in mid flight, already knowing what Crystal's answer would be, she headed across the room to where her pocketbook lay on the floor.

"Do I!" Crystal said eagerly. "Girl let me see...paleeeeeze" She said, extending her hand out for them in anxious anticipation. Tammy grabbed four photos from the side pocket of her bag and walked them over, handing them to Crystal. She looked intently at the first one, studying the young boy's features. He looked to be in his mid-twenties with a dark chocolate complexion and dark brown eyes. He branded a smile as wide as his home continent. His hair was cut in a short taper, very low, almost bald.

"You guys look alike" Crystal said. "What's his name?" she asked.

"Kanye"

"Kanye? Like the rapper Kanye?"

"Yep!" Tammy said, starting her dance routine up again. "It means 'freedom' in the native tongue.

"He's handsome, how old is he?" Crystal asked as she flipped over to the next photo. It was one of Kanye and his mother together.

"He's twenty-four."

" Mmmm hmmm boy what I could do with THAT! Crystal said, taking in his beautiful eyes.

"I swear you're a perve" Tammy said chuckling at her over sexualized friend.

"I'm just saying" Crystal added. "Can't a girl live a little?! And this is your mom right? Afua?" She asked, pointing to the woman in the photo with him.

"Yeah that's her," Tammy said as she leaped across the room. She did a few more twirls on her toes and went to take a seat next to Crystal on the floor.

Crystal was distracted by her heavy breathing. She looked over at Tammy and noticed she was not perspiring. Not a single drop.

"Girl I swear you're a machine!" Crystal said.

"If I got up and did all that stuff you just did, you'd be calling the ambulance." Tammy chuckled. Crystal moved onto the third picture, a family photo. There was a tight lipped man with thick glasses in the photo along with her wide grinned mother and younger brother.

"Is this the *new* man in her life?" Crystal asked.

"Yeah…That's Kanye's father, Jeso. She married him after she returned home. The union was arranged through their parents, before her dad passed over. She told me if she'd been able to decide her own fate, she wouldn't have married him. But not being married after a certain age is frowned upon by the elders in her village. She said she grew to care for him, and he's a great father but that my dad was the one true love of her life."

"So your grandfather did wind up passing away?" Crystal asked.

"Yeah, flip over to the last picture, I'll show you." Crystal took the top photo and placed it at the back of the pile. The last one was of a stately looking gray haired couple, both were neatly dressed, she in her dark blue sailors dress with a strand of white pearls around her neck. Her hair cut short in a neat natural bush, much like Afua's. The man wore a distinguished looking dark grey suit with a black beret' upon his head. The front of it displayed a patch shaped like the continent of Africa. With red, yellow and green stripes and the letters ANC written over it.

"What does that mean?" Crystal pointed.

"That stands for the African National Congress" Tammy replied.

"So your grandfather was a congressman?"

"No. He was part of the military leg of that organization. They fought alongside Nelson and Winnie Mandela."

"Are you serious?!" Crystal stammered in surprise.

"Yep!" Tammy replied proudly.

"Afua said he was a warrior. And that's where she got her fighting spirit from."

"Wow, you got some strong bloodlines girl. Imagine if you would have never met your mom...You wouldn't know *any* of this stuff."

"Yeah, you're so right" Tammy said. As she thought about that.

"He *looks* like he'll kick some ass"...Crystal said. They both laughed at that.

"Sooo when are we going to the Mother Land?" Crystal asked her in a more serious tone. Handing her back the photos. "I know you got a ton of aunties and uncles and cousins that are just dying to meet you...*AND* your little brother! So when we going?"

Tammy smiled at the thought. "Girl, I don't know...I'm still taking all this *innnn.*"

"Well take it in! Take it in girl quick!...Cause I could use a long distance get-a-way...and soon!"

CHAPTER 20

———

CARLOS CRADLED HER LIKE A baby as she lay across his chest. The venetian blinds were drawn open as he watched the sun set from her balcony window. He stroked her curly locks as her eyes rolled to the back of her head in pleasure. She spoke soft and evenly, in a hushed tone as if someone other than the two of them were in the room, as Carlos listened. Every now and again he would grunt, or chuckle to reassure her he was all ears, but nothing more. Stroking her hair gently, he listened patiently to her every word. Tammy went on…

"And my Dad, he can be so clingy. I mean he keeps calling me and I keep telling him over and over again that I'm fine. He's been calling me every three hours. Are you okay, do you need something, you need me to come by?" I be wanting to scream nooooo leave me aloooone!!! I mean I know that he's just trying to protect my feelings but gosh…I'm not three years old any more. You know?" She opened her eyes slightly, looking into his.

"Mmmm hhmmm," Carlos mumbled. His fingers never missing a stroke. She lay with her face toward his chest, her back turned towards the setting sun. Shifting a bit, she maneuvered her body so that her buttocks were protruding out more than before.

"You comfortable" he asked? Preparing himself to adjust his body to her comfort.

"No I'm fine" she said…reassuring him by cuddling up against his body even closer.

She continued... "So then Nana came to see me at the studio yester-day. I didn't even know she was coming, I was like ..."

For the first time since he'd arrived, Carlos lost track of her words. He turned his attention to her body. He watched the way the orange light from the sun's rays landed on the black hip hugger tights she was wearing, he followed the shadowy silloutte up her back. Feeling a bit aroused he reached over her waist and rested his hand on her back side. The rays from the sun now illuminating the back of his hand. Squeezing there gently before moving his fingers up her back.

Tammy knew from that one swift motion what awaited her. It was now a month shy of a year sense they began their courtship, but he was a fast learner. Several weeks after rekindling their relationship, she finally gave into his sexual advances. He knew her body like the back of his hands. He seemed to always know exactly what she wanted, when she wanted it. She kept talking, but her voice got lower as she felt the full weight of his hands upon her body. In one swift gesture he grabbed her inner thigh and pulled firmly, positioning her body to where she was now laying face up across his legs. Tammy loved that about him. Rarely did he ask of her anything...He used his masculine strength to demand what he wanted. As she lay there, flat on her back, face to the sky he went up from the bottom of her fitted tee and began caressing her nipples. Her mouth moments before a motor, now lay silent. Feeling claustropho-bic he slipped his hand out from under.

"Take this off" he commanded. Obeying him without hesitation she sat up and folded her arms in an X across her waist, she grabbed the bot-tom corners of her shirt and pulled it up over her head as he watched. She went to lay back down but he placed his hand on her back, stopping her.

"Take the bra off too" he said hungrily. She reached around and snapped the eyehooks off her bra, pulling it away from her body she allowed it to drop to the floor. She lay back, her bare skin touching the jean on his pant legs. He sat there for a moment, taking her body in with his eyes.

"*So Beautiful*" he said, speaking more to himself than her. He took his finger and traced it from her neck slowly down to her belly button. He used his hands to cup her perfectly round breast squeezing gently at the nipples. She let out a sharp whence of pleasure, arching her back in response. He took his hands and placed them on her back near her shoulder blades. He hoisted her up closer to his chest and took as much of her breast as he could get into his mouth, sucking gently. Her eyes rolled to the back of her head as she lay there lifeless. He owned every piece of her in that moment. After a few had passed, he repeated the same motion on her other breast, this time biting down softly on her nipple.

"Ceeeee," she allowed the word to ooze out of her mouth. Passion filling the air like thick smog. He used his strength to lift her body up higher and slipped beneath her off the couch, laying her back down gently. He stood up, walking around to the end of the couch where her bare feet lay, he grabbed one foot and began sucking her toes. She groaned with delight. After tasting them enough, he reached for her legs, sitting them up into a knee bent position. He kneeled on the couch between her legs and grabbed at the elastic on her waist pants, pulling at it roughly. Her panties coming along for the ride he took the loose clothing and tossed them on top of the growing pile on the floor. She now lay naked, helplessly naked, nothing left to protect her from his animal instincts. Still kneeling between her legs he took one hand and cupped her breast. He used the other and began gently caressing her clit. She bit her bottom lip, trying desperately to hold back the noises rising up from her throat.

"*Oh God*" she whispered softly. Carlos was bone hard, but he didn't let that interfere with the moment. Watching her in so much pleasure made his heart race faster.

"*Oh God*" she said again through groans as he thrust his middle finger up in her and began wiggling it. He leaned in, kissing her lips. Softly at first and then taking his tongue and forcing it in her mouth. They remained like that, tongue tied, breath held, riding on pure emotion for what seemed like a lifetime before he snatched his body up away from hers, eyeing her wetness he leaned down and put all of his tongue in between her legs. She arched her back, her body unable to withstand the powerful force of his own. She moved her hips to get away from his mouth but his neck followed her every sway. She flopped back down to the sofa, defenseless against his forceful passion. Remembering where she was, she slid her bottom off the couch onto the cold wood floor. He followed her down, they both put a hand on the magazine table pushing it out the way. The wooden legs making a thug noise as it slid across the floor.

His tongue went back between her legs. She scratched at his back, trying to pull his shirt up from over his neck. As he lift his head to help her she scooted her body down toward his crotch. Feeling the same sense of urgency to please him as he did her she quickly maneuvered the zipper on his jeans like a surgeon. She didn't have to go looking for what she wanted; it was protruding strongly through his pants. She reached in and grabbed him, placing all of him in her mouth, his firm body went limp.

"Ooooh baby," he said, resting his hip between the floor and the couch his head dropped like a junkie taking his first hit. He lay there, weak, allowing her to please every part of his senses. He let her go on like that until his body couldn't withstand another second. He rose up to straddle her, full to the brim with life for her. He reached down and grabbed himself. She shifted her body to prepare herself openly and willingly to accept him. In that brief moment their eyes locked, both staring deep down into the window of the others soul. In that moment they were one, a single source, locked together in a cage of hunger and thirst.

"*I love you so much*" she whispered, right before he forced himself inside of her.

CHAPTER 21

———◆———

CARLOS WAS SURPRISED TRE HAD confided so much in him. He wasn't quite comfortable with it, especially with the secrets he held deep in his own soul.

"Damn man....I'm sorry to hear that." He said as he reached in the bag of chips in front of him, pulling out a handful and popping them into his mouth . . . Not having much more than that to add to the discussion. They were in the studio having a late lunch. They worked through breakfast and right into late afternoon before Tre buzzed the booth to tell Carlos to come out and grub with him.

"I KNOW you've got to be as hungry as I am Cee?" Come on man... I had Miss Barb order us some food from the corner deli...It's here." Carlos was grateful for the break AND the food. He'd been surviving on noodles and canned tuna for the last week. Fresh deli sandwiches were music to his ears. He was enjoying the meal, but the conversation he could've done without. Tre continued, grateful to have a listening ear.

"So now I have to give these greedy cocksuckers fifty g's...FIFTY G's man!!! Just like that! It's either that or a jury trial." Carlos didn't see the need for all the frustration. He thought if he were in Tre's shoes, he'd just go on and pay the money without hesitation. Especially if it was a problem that he himself created. But Carlos spoke none of this aloud. He made a mental note that when he started raking in the dough, he wouldn't be so tight with his money like a lot of these other big wads. Carlos had plans for his money, and they didn't include filling up on fancy luxuries, getting high on materialism. No. He planned to take MOST of the money he made and give it back to the youth. He figured if he could save other young men from following the same troubled path he did, he had the responsibility and duty to make that happen.

"So how's Crystal, is she doing alright?" This was the moment Carlos was dreading. It's why he never wanted to buddy up to him in the first place. He felt like a... "phony."

Carlos just shook his head yeah, before taking a long swig of his half empty cup of iced tea. He had hoped his mouth full of food would halt the flow of discussion. "What about Tammy have you seen her? Those two are inseparable, I'm sure you have huh?" Tre prodded. Not waiting on an answer he continued,

"Damn I miss that girl." Tre said, as he turned to reach for a napkin at the opposite end of the table. None too soon as the look of contempt on Carlos's face would've been a dead give-a-way. "I mean she got the whole package." Tre went on... "beauty, brains . . . that ass . . . I would pay top dollar just to..."

"Man I'm done!" Carlos said as he stood up sharply, slamming the balled up napkin he held tightly in his fist down on the table. Tre shot him a look of total confusion.

"What?" he asked.

"Nothing, I'm just done. Are we gonna finish up that last track or what?" Carlos spat . . . squaring his shoulders as if he was preparing for battle. Tre thought to himself for a second before responding.

"What the hell is wrong with you? Are you fucking bipolar or something?"

Carlos looked him square in the eye. His mind teetering back and forth with the thought of telling him....or not. Carlos was tired of the charade, his soul wanted out of the lie, but he wasn't sure if this was the proper time to release it . . . or was it? Easing the tension in his shoulders, he opened his mouth to speak and then quickly shut it back again. Tre noticing the look of confusion on his face.

"What the *hell* is wrong with you?" he asked again. Just then Tre's cell phone rang. He reached down to retrieve it and Carlos never felt more relief in his life. Tre stood up to take the call in his office as Carlos took that opportunity to make his way towards the window on the opposite side of the room. Putting some distance between them.

"Well, well, well, long time no hear from" he could hear Tre saying right before his voice trailed off into the back office. Carlos fiddled around with some lyrics he had stored in his head, bopping to the sound of an invisible beat, attempting to find his focus again. He was still sitting on the high stool staring out the window when Tre swung open his office door ten minutes later. The move was so sudden that it startled Carlos. He turned around to see a ghost! Tre's dark brown skin had turned pale, his eyes wide as saucers.

"Wassup man?" Carlos looked concerned for him as he stood up from the stool. Tre walked slowly over to his sound equipment, moving like he'd aged fifty years in ten minutes. He took a seat behind the board, looking past Carlos and through the wall, his mind still on the conversation that had just taken place inside that office.

"Aye maaan, you don't look so hot. You need me to call somebody?" Finally after a long pause Tre looked at him. Carlos could see fear in his eyes.

"I fucked that girl bare and she got AIDS!"...

———◀▶———

CHAPTER 22

TAMMY HELD HER HAND OVER her mouth in total shock while Carlos continued with the details of what he knew. "…and then he started cursing and kicking stuff. He went off up in there. He kicked over the trash can, stuff flew everywhere. I felt so bad for the dude, I aint know what to say." Crystal and Reds sat in the booth across from them, she shook her head in disgust. They were at their usual hang out spot, Ray's bar and grill where they all met together for the first time a year earlier. Reds was chewing on a mozzarella stick they'd ordered for appetizers, no one around the table seemed to have an appetite at that moment except for him.

"That's a shame" Crystal blurted. "I can't believe he'd be so stupid to risk his life like that."

"What did he say he was gonna do?" Tammy asked, edging Carlos on for more details.

"I suggested he go get tested right away…like TONIGHT! He said he was gonna go in the morning, he looked scared as shit when I left.

"*Scared!*" Tammy stammered. "Oh my God I wouldn't know *what* to do with myself. Aww man I feel so bad for him," she said under her breath. Carlos felt a pang of jealousy hit him. He knew he had Tammy's heart, in spite of, he still wasn't cool with her feeling "anything" for Tre . . . not even sorry.

"That mess aint no joke," Reds chimed in before dipping another stick in the marinara sauce, popping the whole thing in his mouth.

Crystal looked at him in disgust. "I can't believe you still have an appetite after listening to all this!"

"*What?*" He responded grinning. "What you expect *me* to do?" Y'all prolly all worried for nothing anyways, he said between chews. "Just because *she* got it, don't mean he automatically gonna catch it too."

"That's a good point, Carlos said. There is that chance of him escaping a bullet. I'd sure nuff be losing my mind until I found out though."

"Oh My God," Tammy repeated. "This makes me so grateful that you and I got tested together, before…." "Yeah, me too." Carlos agreed, placing his hand on her thigh under the table for moral support.

"Who is she?" Crystal asked Carlos. He shrugged his shoulders.

"I dunno, some chick he was messin around with a few months back. I mean I didn't ask him no details, I think he was just needing somebody to listen, you know. I was sympathetic to the dude, but I aint go all into details like y'all women be doing."

"I know right!" Reds said still chewing. "Y'all be wanting to know what the weather was outside when they did the do…what kinda jewelry she was wearing, what food they ate . . . all that." Reds laughed all by himself. Crystal shot him a look that was even more disgusting than before.

"I don't see what's so funny about all this?" she said, her tone of voice matching the expression on her face. Both women had their fair share of drama when it came to Tre, but they loved him none-the-less, he was a friend.

"Oh my God" Tammy repeated for the umpteenth time. Ignoring the tension across the table. "I feel like I should call him or something?"

"Call him for what?" It was Carlos's turn to feel irritated. "I mean, I know I can't *mention* what you just told us, but still, I feel like he may need somebody right now. I couldn't imagine the stress he must be under right now."

"Why *you* gotta call him? Why can't Crystal call him or something?" Crystal and Tammy gave each other a knowing look, they understood without having to exchange words what Carlos was feeling.

Crystal answered, "I can call him, but he'd be more appreciative if she called him I'm sure. I'm sorry Carlos, I know this must make you feel kinda awkward but gosh, the man might be dying for Christ sakes!" Carlos thought about what she had said. He knew he shouldn't be so jealous, especially at a time like this, but he couldn't help himself. He fought with his emotions, fighting over wanting Tre to have some sort of comfort but not with his woman involved. He reminded himself that they were all friends before he came on the scene. It was his good nature that helped to settle his inner battle.

"You're right" He said. "You're absolutely right." Babe if you think it would help to give him a call, you have my blessing." But don't you be settin up no face to face meetings with him" he added, pointing a finger at her face.

"Don't be leading him on no kinda way!"

"Boy hush!" Tammy said smacking her teeth, pushing his finger away. "Why would I do *that*?" The waitress came to take their orders, but they were so wrapped up into the discussion none of them were prepared. Carlos sent her away, asking that she give them a few more minutes to look over the menu.

"I don't even have an appetite no more" Crystal said, looking over the menu in front of her. Tammy leaned further against the back of the booth, she was heavy in thought. She didn't even try hiding her emotions. This news was devastating to her. She surprised herself at the level of emotion she was feeling about it. She silently prayed for his well being, she did not want to see him hurt.

"I hope he's gonna be alright" she whispered aloud. Carlos looked up from his menu into her face. He never felt so jealous of another person in his life. He stared intently into her eyes, peering into her soul. He wasn't sure what it was he was feeling…insecurity…hurt….disdain….He just knew that what he saw through her eyes, wasn't comforting.

———◆———

Tre sat in the exam room where he'd come through the back door, bypassing those sitting in the waiting area. With his clout, he could do these type of things with no questions asked. This was the second visit Tre had with this particular doctor. He was there once before for a bad ear infection he'd caught early upon arriving in the city from Texas. Doc told him that it was possibly caused by the drastic change in weather patterns from one coast to the other. He was using head-phones regularly in the damp fog during his early morning jogging sprints. This was before more people began to recognize who he was. The dew mixed with the heat of his breath could've caused moisture to seep through. The Doc was helpful and friendly, a brother. Somebody Tre took to immediately. They chatted then about his move and the vast difference in their career paths, it was an intelligent conversation. Tre felt right about coming back here, to see him. He knew he was taking a chance with a press leak just for being there, but he couldn't escape chance all the time. He sat there on the exam table thinking about his life choices while he waited on the Doc to return with the equipment he'd need to draw blood. He could've allowed his nurse to handle his prep work, but Tre was a high profile patient, the Doc thought it best if he handled it all himself.

Tre sat there thinking about his mom, how she'd feel if the news was bad. He thought about not having any children. How he always wanted a son and what this meant for his future dreams of having a family. He was kicking himself over and over again for being so weak for Sherry to-wards the end of their . . . their fling. He started out wearing a condom with her every time they'd have sex, as he always did with other random women he slept with. But after days turned to weeks, and weeks turned into months and they were still seeing each other, things began to get sloppy. He knew it was stupid of him when he did it, both times, having sex with that woman without protection. He was reacting to lust, his lower senses, which overrode his logical senses. He felt like an idiot. All the things he worked for, all the successes he achieved in his life, lead up to this one horrific moment; sitting painstakingly on the doctors table waiting on another man, a stranger of sorts, to give him the results of his life's fate.

He felt like crying. He would never do it, not out in public, not like this, but he felt like it. Just then the doctor burst into the room not bothering to knock. He carried with him two syringes, a thick rubber band and several multi-sized glass tubes with different color rubber caps at the ends. Doc was a distinguished looking man. His greyish black hair looked noble up against his crisp white coat. The coat was pressed neatly, his pen and temperature gaze poking out from the front top pocket. He reached over and grabbed a pair of plastic gloves from the box on the counter along with two pre-packaged alcohol swabs and some cotton balls. Tre noticed a wedding band on his finger. A simple rounded edged gold wedding band. He thought for a moment how much easier the Doc's life must be in comparison to his own. How living in the fast lane had its material advantages yes, but it also carried with it some dark moments. Selfish, greedy and careless dark moments. He wished in that brief moment he and the Doc could switch places.

"It'll take us up to five days to get these results back. Unfortunately, you won't know right away, but soon enough" he said, placing the thick rubber band around Tre's arm to assist him in finding a proper vein.

"Doc let me ask you something, what goes through your mind when you see a man like me, in my situation come through your door?" Doc looked up at him briefly to determine if he was joking or not as he wiped the crease in Tre's arm with the wet cotton swab . . .

Tre continued... "I mean, I know you've seen your fair share of patients in my same situation, what do you think about us?" The Doctor took a few seconds to mull over his words before speaking.

"Why do you ask?" he said, right before sticking Tre's arm with the needle. Tre didn't even flinch.

"I'm just curious," he said. Tre wasn't sure why he asked the question, other than the fact that he was in a mood to torture his own soul. He was disappointed in himself, and in some twisted way he was looking to the doctor to punish him for his sins.

"Well...yes, you're correct, I have seen my share of men...both men *and women*...come through these doors in similar circumstances, but I don't make a habit of judging my patients." He pulled the first tube out and put another in its place.

"I can respect that" Tre said looking down at his arm. Not completely satisfied with the answer he pushed further...

"I'm not asking you to judge Doc, I just wanna know your perspective, you know. What do you be thinking as you take blood from folks like *me*?" He placed emphasis on the last word. He spoke it as if he thought of himself as a walking plague, scum of the earth. The Doctor understood his attempts, deciding upon another route he told him . . .

"I wouldn't beat myself up about it if I were you champ. You don't know what the outcome will be. If I were you, I'd be looking at the bright side. Your worries may be in vain." Tre knew he was right, but it made him feel no less pleased with himself. His sorrows went deeper than the outcome of the test. He was feeling some kinda way about the circumstances of his life that placed him in this predicament to begin with. Despite all his outward successes, he felt empty inside.

The Doctor reached over and placed both tubes of blood onto a holding tray. He grabbed a dry cotton ball and placed it on the spot where the needle had exited.

"Bend your arm" he said. Tre did as asked. He reached back onto the desk and grabbed a band-aid.

"I'll call you myself when the test results return. The lab has to conduct a western blot, this takes a while longer than usual so don't get excited if you haven't heard from me in a few days. I know it's hard to do but try not to worry yourself so much about it. You should go out, spend some time with friends this week, they'll remind you of how much more life you have in you...REGARDLESS of the outcome".

Tre thought about his words, he searched his mind for some friendly faces he could call, but there was only one. The thought of Tammy made him feel even worse than before.

"Thanks Doc" he said, standing up from the table. Both men knew it wouldn't be any pleasantries to hang around and chat about today. Besides the sooner Tre got out of there, the less chance that he'd be seen.

"Wait here a sec" the Doc said. Let me check the hall to be sure the coast is clear." He opened the exam room door and stepped out, closing it halfway behind him. After a few seconds he reached his hand back into the room, waving him to come on out.

Tre left as quietly as he had entered. He slipped out the back door used for loading. He placed his dark shades on his face as he eased into the back of the waiting Mercedes.

———▶———

Tre had the driver take him to "The Rooftop at Annie's." A well-known soul food restaurant across the city in Brooklyn. Tre first met Annie through Mike, the restauranteur community was small in New York City for black owners so they all knew of each other some way, somehow.

Annie operated her restaurant from the rooftop of a twelve story building, which sat mostly empty during the early morning hours, which is exactly why Tre chose to go there in the first place. He enjoyed being up high, in places far above the ground but didn't want to go back to his own studio apartment. He figured he'd use the fresh morning air to clear his head. As he arrived a few workers were mulling around filling empty ketchup bottles, wiping smudge marks off the bar glasses. A few others were back in the kitchen area, preparing dishes no doubt for the day's customers who were sure to come. With the exception of these workers Tre had the rooftop all to himself. He took a seat on one of the wait benches nearest to the rooftop railing, placing both feet up on the chair across from him. He tilted his head back against the rail, face up to the sky, he closed his eyes, allowing his thoughts to take over....It was a chilly morning to be out without a jacket, but the chill was the farthest thing from his fragile mind at that moment. He sat quietly listening to the loud honks from the passing cabbies' horns too in a hurry to wait. And the screeching brakes from the busses stopping to pick up passengers at the corner below. He kept shaking his head, back and forth, still not fully accepting the fact that he was here, right here at this point in his life. His cell phone rang. Startled by the rarest of sound, he opened his eyes, quickly sitting up straight. He knew from the ring tone that it was Tammy calling. Her number was attached to one of the first songs he'd ever recorded, entitled "my first love". It was a catchy tune that never did take off. He could hide behind what the song meant to him without anyone ever picking up on it, and yet still experience the excitement every time she called. He gathered himself before answering.

"Hello". . . he was nervous with anticipation.

"Tre!" Tammy shouted in a tone more chipper than usually reserves for him.

"What you doing?" she added.

"Aaaah I'm just chilling at the moment. What the hell are you doing?" He asked playfully.

"Nothing, I haven't heard from you in a couple of weeks, so I thought I'd call, to make sure you weren't dead or something..." Tre's mind raced. He knew this was out of character for Tammy to just call him out the blue...for nothing in particular. He thought about the conversation he had with Carlos at the studio the day before, and began putting two and two together. He decided to play along, just in case his thoughts weren't accurate.

"Well as you can hear, I'm alive. So what you want? My body or something?" He thought about what he just said, a sharp pang went through his heart.

"Boy eeeew, would you stop it, nobody wants you like that. I'm just . . . calling that's all . . . as a friend. Checking up on you to make sure you're okay?"

The way she said it left Tre with no further doubt that she knew. He found himself becoming angry at Carlos for spilling the beans.

"I'm alright…why? You gonna save me or something?" he shot back in an even tone. Tammy sensed the defense rising up in his voice, she decided to take the compassionate route with him.

"No I'm not gonna *save* you, she said softly. But as your friend, I'm gonna be there when you need me." Tre's heart melted. These were the reasons he felt so much for her. She could melt his icy heart with just one sentence.

"Well I need you now" he said, in a much gentler tone than before.

"I could really use a friend." He closed his eyes, feeling his way through. He knew he was taking a chance exposing his emotions to her, he was raw, wide open, but he didn't care. He was taking a chance at his feelings getting crushed, but he didn't care. Tammy sensed the desperation in his voice.

"Where are you?" she asked him.

"I'm sitting here, at Annie's Rooftop over in Brooklyn."

Tammy thought about Carlos, what he said to her…"*don't be having no face-to-face meetings with him.*" She had no intentions on disobeying her man, but a friend needed her.

She played with the thought back and forth in her mind, torn, before finally responding, "I'm on my way."

CHAPTER 23

WHEN TAMMY ARRIVED THIRTY MINUTES later, Tre was sitting in the same position he was when he hung up from her. He appeared to be sleeping so she tip-toed over in an effort to scare him. She got close enough to reach down and shake him by the collar but he wasn't sleeping, not by a longshot. He felt her presence and right before she could grab his collar, he reached out and yanked her by the waist, pulling her down on top of him playfully. Tammy let out a high pitched yelp.

"You bastard!" she said punching him in the chest with her fist. He laughed heartily as she attempted to pull away.

"Let me go silly and where is your coat?" she said. But Tre resisted. He held on to her tighter, half joking, half seriously needing someone he loved close to him. She insisted he let her go, squealing all the while. He didn't want the mood to become awkward so finally he released her from his grip. Tammy took a moment to gather herself, looking around at the open space. "How'd you manage to get this place all to yourself?" she asked him. Placing her purse on the bench beside him.

"Connects" was his reply.

"What you doing over here in Brooklyn coming to see me this morning? Don't you got some young dancers you can beat up on today?"

"I don't *beat up* on my dancers, she said rolling her eyes, taking a seat beside him. No, I don't have any *classes*, not until later this evening."

"Hmmm" he responded, studying her pretty face.

"Tell me what you know!" He said sharply. He never was one to beat around the bush, it just wasn't his style. Tammy looked over at him, realizing at that moment he knew, she knew. She decided not to play any games with the information.

"I know that you have some heavy news weighing on you. And I know that you're gonna be okay no matter what." They gazed into each other's eyes for longer than a moment. Finally, he smiled and reached over to give her a big bear hug.

"I love you Tammy – you know that?" They were the sincerest words he ever said to a woman.

"I love you too, she said" as they remained locked in an embrace longer than Carlos would ever be comfortable with.

"Did you eat?" she finally asked him, pulling away and standing up. Tre had to think about if he had or not . . .

"Naaah", he said.

"Well how's the food at this place? She asked, steering the mood away from somber.

"Who do I need to see to get us some food around here? Where's your *connects*?" She asked jokingly. Tre smiled defenselessly up at her. He was in no mood to eat, but in no mood to stop her either. He allowed her to lead. He pointed towards the steps...

"Annie's around here someplace. Go down a flight and one of her staffers will point her out to you." Tammy turned and walked off in the direction of his finger. She returned fifteen minutes later with one of the waiters in tow. He carried a large metal tray with a silver dome top on his shoulder. Tre really did fall asleep this time, so she reached over, gently shaking his leg while the waiter placed the tray on a table closest to him.

"Will this be all Madame?" He asked as he stood there waiting for a reply.

:Yes...yes...thank you so so much Eddie for accommodating us. Please give my thanks again to the chef." Tre stretched as he sat up on the bench.

"Come over and eat something," she told him. It's chilly up here, can you turn that thing on?" Pointing to one of the tall outdoor heat lamps sitting near the corner of the patio. Tre went over and pulled it closer to where they sat, turning it up on full blast before sitting down next to her at the table.

"What you got?" he asked curious as she pulled the top off the tray.

It looked as if she'd raided the refrigerator. She had small sample bowls of just about everything on the menu. Collard greens, corn, sweet potatoes, cabbage, potato salad, corn bread, macaroni and cheese...

"Where's the meat??" Tre asked in defiance.

"Boy you don't need no meat. If you can't get full off all this, something's wrong with you." She grabbed one of the empty plates and began scooping half of what was in each bowl onto it. He sat back watching her, wishing at that moment they were somewhere in their own home, she serving a meal she had cooked for him, exclusively for him. Just then Eddie the waiter's voice snapped him out of his daydream, he was carrying two glass mugs on a small tray.

"I almost forgot, here's your tea."

"Tea!" Tre said disappointedly. Is that a *long island* tea? He asked him. Tammy chimed in . . . "Don't pay him no mind Eddie, thank you so much you can set them right there.

Tre shook his head in disapproval but saying nothing more. He was enjoying this interaction with her. As he watched her prepare their plates, he thought of how he could get used to this. He wanted to reach over and kiss her cheek, or stroke her hair or rub her thigh...something! He wanted to be nearer to her, closer, but he thought he better not push it... so he sat there instead, watching intently her every move, studying her body movements like a lion would his prey.

"You haven't eaten *anything* today?" She asked.

"No" He shot back...watching her wrist as they delicately scooped each spoonful of food onto his plate. Her every move was a sensual dance. He found himself becoming emotional by how vulnerable he was for her. Just then anger swept over him, he felt angry for wanting something so bad he could not have.

"That's enough" he said, his jaw clenching.

"What?" she responded in surprise… "But you gotta try this…"

"I said that's enough," he repeated sternly. She shot him a look of confusion. "Okay okay…don't bite my head off gosh." She took the plate and sat it in front of him, then picked up the other empty plate and began to fill her own. He turned his attention over to the food, not waiting he began eating.

"Aren't you gonna say grace?" She asked.

"You say it for me," was his reply as he heaped a forkful of macaroni and cheese into his mouth. Tammy sat her plate in front of her, placed her hands down to her side and closed her eyes. She whispered a small prayer of thanks for the both of them. Tre's fork never missed a beat.

"Did you even say Amen, Ase or *something*?" She asked teasingly.

He grinned a sly grin and spoke through clinched teeth…. "I knew you had me." Tammy laughed light heartedly, shaking her head in disgrace before grabbing her own fork from the table. They sat there in silence, enjoying the meal, the heat from the lamp and each other's company. After finishing his plate and going in for seconds, Tre sat back and grabbed his tight stomach with both hands.

"Damn, I aint even realize I was that hungry."

"You did eat a LOT of food greedmo" Tammy said, wiping her mouth with the napkin before placing it on the table beside her half eaten plate.

"Did you like the food?" He asked.

"Oh yes! Cryss and I will be back here for sure. I know she'll like it. As much as I don't wanna, I *gotta* be careful eating so much of this kinda food.

"What you tryna rid yourself of your soulfulness? You bougie now?" He said, nudging her shoulder playfully to drive home his point.

"Ha!" Tammy laughed out loud…. "Never that!" But have you seen some of my "*soul* sista's walking around here lately? I'll take the soul but they can keep the food." It was Tre's turn to laugh.

"I can't even picture you being a big girl." He said looking down at her waist. Her thin wool overcoat nicely tapered on both sides.

"And you never will!" Tammy said, emphasizing her words with a smirk. Tre loved it when she moved her mouth like that. She reminded him of a porcelain doll. So valuable and fragile. He liked everything about her. It's why he could not get past her. Every time he tried envisioning her as just another random chick who understood the game, she'd crush those thoughts with one smirk of the face.

"Tammy why do you refuse to give us a chance?" His words cutting through the light hearted air like a sledge hammer. He didn't even think on what he was saying, he just spoke from the heart. He knew he was entering unchartered territory, but something about the moment, gave him the courage to go further....

"Don't you know by now how I *feel* about you? Don't you know that I wanna give you the world?" Tammy cut his words short..."Tre let's not do this okay? We're here, enjoying this nice meal, and..."

"Tammy cut the crap!" he blurted irritably. *Stop* trying to protect my feelings. "Talk to *me!*" he said pleadingly. *"Tell me why you won't give us a chance?"* It was in that moment, Tammy knew it was gonna be *now* that she told him. She looked him square in the eye. The same feeling to come over her that night at the album release party came rushing back. She wasn't sure what it was she was feeling. Lust, compassion, loyalty . . . maybe a mixture of them all? She looked down and began fiddling with a piece of lint on her pant leg. Thinking hard on what she should say next.

"After all these years, do you not know how much I care for you? What I wouldn't *do* for you?" He pushed.

She looked up at him again, and then away. Staring out into the fog-filled sky, far into the distance.

"Tre you and I are *worlds* apart. She whispered. Our lifestyles are *totally* different in every way. There's no way we could ever be truly happy together.

"But how do you *know?*" He said gently. Sitting up straighter in his chair. All his health worries went out the window in that moment.

Sensing he had an opening into the conversation he's been dying to have with her for years, he took full advantage and pressed on...

"I know we come from two different backgrounds. But I *swear* I could be the man you need me to be, I *know* I can. Let me show you..."

"Tre, Carlos and I are dating. And we have been for a year, and I love him, and would never want to see him hurt." Tre was clearly startled. His mind went racing. It took him several moments to gather his thoughts.

"Carlos?... *Who?*... Cee!...You mean *Cee-Los?*" He spat the words out in pure disgust.

She looked him square in his eyes, and without her needing to utter another word, he had his answer. Tre scooted his chair back from the table in one swift motion, needing to distance himself from the source of his pain. He stood up turning his back on her, he walked briskly towards the far end of the rooftop and grabbed ahold of the rail tightly, looking down at the street below.

Tammy got up and walked over to where he stood. She placed one hand gently on his elbow, and spoke softly..."Tre...I never meant...."

He yanked his arm away forcefully, and without removing his gaze from the streets below he spoke sharply...

"So you and Cee been fucking all this time huh?"

AL-QAMAR MALIK IS AN ENTREPRENEUR and popular social justice blogger. She grew up in Washington, DC, and currently lives in Fort Washington, Maryland. She has two adult children.

A lifelong writer, this is Al-Qamar's first published novel.